THE COTSWOLD CONNECTION

Drugs investigator Mike O'Hara visits a small Cotswold village following a tip-off that this region could be the source of a new heroin-based drug known as Mega-H. This doctored heroin is far more addictive and dangerous than the normal drug. Soon after his arrival, O'Hara discovers the body of a murdered girl. Thus begins the unfolding of a story of brutal murder, ruthless drug-dealing villains, torture and family intrigue.

CHARLES JACKSON

THE COTSWOLD CONNECTION

Complete and Unabridged

LINFORD
Leicester

First published in Great Britain in 1984

Originally published under the name
'Charles Vivian'

First Linford Edition
published 1997
by arrangement with
Bookland Company Limited
Enfield
Middlesex

Copyright © 1984 by Charles Vivian
All rights reserved

British Library CIP Data

Jackson, Charles
 The Cotswold connection.—Large print ed.—
Linford mystery library
 1. Thrillers
 2. Large type books
 I. Title
 823.9'12 [F]

ISBN 0–7089–5072–8

Published by
F. A. Thorpe (Publishing) Ltd.
Anstey, Leicestershire

Set by Words & Graphics Ltd.
Anstey, Leicestershire
Printed and bound in Great Britain by
T. J. Press International Ltd., Padstow, Cornwall

This book is printed on acid-free paper

Author's Note

The locale of this story is an amalgam of many features of the delightful Cotswold scene. It is possible that some readers may think to recognise various fragments of the scenario, despite certain topographical liberties which have been taken.

However, while there may well be hotel managers, police inspectors, blaspheming baronets, illegitimate sons, eminent judges, and even the odd drug baron or so residing in the Cotswolds, may I assure readers that all characters in this story — especially the villainous ones — are purely figments of imagination and bear no resemblance to living persons.

The brief account of those Opium Warlords, Lo Sing Han and his rival, Kun Sar, both of whom tried to treat with the U.S. Government, offering to destroy their considerable opium harvests for an equally considerable payment is, however, fact and not fiction.

Unfortunately, trafficking in illegal drugs is such a lucrative proposition these days that the number of addicts escalates year by year. Few of us fully realise the immense damage being done to the youth of our civilized world by those unscrupulous enough to exploit addictive appetites for, often, enormous monetary gains.

C.J.

1

THE good fortune of the O'Haras is a noted phenomenon — because of its marked infrequency!

There are some who blame this on slow horses and fast women, while others argue that while seventh sons of seventh sons should have a lot going for them, that lot's not always in the right direction. Whatever the reason, Lady Luck leers as often as she smiles on this scion of the O'Hara clan. I've often thought that if only the good Lady would come out from the undergrowth and reveal herself I might be able to charm her with my winsome ways — the dear old Dad didn't take me along to kiss the Blarney Stone for nothing.

Now take today, as far as it's gone: I wish you would because I've already had more than enough of it. This morning I landed up in a perfectly reasonable hotel at Upper Chilworth, that straggling but picturesque Cotswold village encircling a valley which, naturally enough, I suppose, is the site for Lower Chilworth. Having parked my MG Sports, then signed in and collected my key at the reception desk in the hotel foyer, I decided that a lift to the first floor was for lesser mortals and hefted my luggage up the polished pine stairway.

I had been allocated room 12A by the powers that be of the Bellevue Hotel, and such is the sway of superstition that I found my room flanked by numbers 12 and 14. Now I would have been perfectly happy with a room numbered 13. Today happens to be Mrs. O'Hara's youngest son Michael's birthday: it's June the 13th wouldn't you know! As I hove to by the door of my room I fell to wondering just what little treat I could afford myself on this day of days. I may be the baby son of the family and the pride in my mother's eyes, but it was an undeniable fact that I had now clocked up well over thirty odd summers — some of them very odd, but few as odd as this one, as I was due to discover!

Like many hotel door-locks, the one securing Room 12A presented its own complex little problem. A few terse words later I perceived that the key and the door-knob turned together in one smooth combination, thus gaining me entrance to a clean if somewhat austerely furnished room. There was a close-boarded pine floor with rugs placed at strategic points flanking the bedside and fronting the dressing-table; white walls bearing a couple of hunting prints; a pale blue ceiling laced in one corner with a web of fine cracks which widened as it started into the coving and coursed down the wall for half-a-metre or so, and immediately brought the word subsidence to my mind; some plain but functional furniture of mock Scandinavian design; the whole offset by rather garish blue curtains and bed-cover — and all this to be home for the next week or so.

Heaving my scuffed old suitcase on to the low, slatted table I judged to be designed for this chore, I dropped an equally worn airways bag on to a handy chair — the only chair that the room boasted — and parted the curtains to allow the late morning sun to dapple the room as it filtered through the bosky branches of the magnificent beech-tree in the garden outside. My next, and rather pressing port of call — a couple of pints of bitter at a hospitable and ancient hostelry in Burford, you understand — was the combined toilet-bathroom positioned as a separate cubicle immediately to the right-hand side of the room entrance.

The room was clean enough, and like the furniture was gratifyingly functional. But once the pressures of my recent journey had been relieved and my hands and face refreshingly doused in cold water, I became aware of the nagging sound of a steadily dripping tap. I gave both taps at the wash-basin, the hot as well as the cold tap a turn for good measure. With the sound of dripping water still persisting, I turned to the bath which was completely curtained by a heavy blue-and-white patterned plastic. This slid easily aside at the leisurely sweep of my hand — and there she lay, appearing to shimmer slightly beneath the surface.

The poor girl was as nude as a peeled banana. An obviously natural blonde whose voluptuous young body was quite, quite cold to the touch, while a close examination revealed bruised throttle-marks showing up as an obscene necklace about her slim white throat.

Panic-stricken I was not. Curious — certainly! In my latter-day profession (not an everyday sort of a job I'll readily admit) violent death was no stranger although never to be encouraged, of course.

Immediate assistance was of no

earthly use to the blonde now, so I cast around to see what traces there were of her former occupancy of Room 12A — at the same time thinking that since Lady Luck was never fooled, the hotel people might just as well have kept the room at its true 13.

Although I searched that room with a diligence of which Holmes and Watson would have approved I found nothing untoward. No clothing. No cosmetics. Not a thing in the wardrobe or the dressing-chest. Nothing in the bedside cabinet and nothing under the bed, apart from a mild accumulation of fluff. In fact, there was not a single trace in that room that spoke of her earlier presence — not even a single blonde hair.

Apart from her body there was the same lack of evidence in the bathroom. No clothing. No toiletries. Not even splashings on the tiled floor to mark a struggle of thrashing limbs while she was striving to avoid being choked or drowned. Another more careful scrutiny elicited no significantly identifying detail on her body, other than a neat, well-healed appendectomy scar on the lower right-hand side of a cute little abdomen. There was no jewellery; no nail-polish on the sensitive slender-fingered hands; but there were the incriminating marks of the regular use of a hypodermic needle on her left fore-arm.

A couple of crude Anglo-Saxon expletives escaped me at sight of those needle-marks. This was far from being the first time I had seen victims of drug addiction. Among so very many others, my own sister had finally succumbed to the habit after leading a hellishly tortured existence because of her dependency on heroin. It had been my vengeful delight to ensure that the particular drug-pusher who had helped to speed her to an early death, by trafficking in a heroin-based concoction that had been laced with some other vile additive muck, came to a stickily unpleasant end himself — but too late to save little sister, Maureen.

I bent over the bath again to examine the blonde. I realized that the regular use of a hypo-needle could have been the necessary medication for something like diabetes, but the sixth sense of this seventh son suggested that it was not so in this case. Although, I had to admit that whatever she had been injecting herself with had so far caused no emaciation or apparent physical deterioration of a remarkably nubile young body.

Realizing that it was time for me to set certain wheels in motion, I re-entered the bedroom and crossed to where the bedside cabinet sported a telephone.

"I need the manager up here in Room 12A straightaway, please!"

"But — but, sir . . ." a voice burbled back over the 'phone.

"No ifs, no buts — and certainly no procrastination," I said curtly. "Let's have him up here immediately, but warn him to be prepared for a shock!"

"Really, sir, this *is* the manager speaking," the voice had now stopped burbling and had adopted a pseudo huntin', fishin' and shootin' tone. "Is the matter so very urgent? You see I have to make certain arrangements with the chef. We shall soon have to start serving luncheon."

"I'm sure you'll find this much more important than any luncheon arrangements can be — "

"I can scarcely believe that, sir ... Now if it's a question of more bed-linen that you require — or perhaps the maid has forgotten to leave towels in the bathroom ... "

"You're getting quite warm, old son," I replied. "The source of the trouble is certainly in the bathroom. You'll find the matter quite traumatic, I shouldn't wonder. Guaranteed to rock you back on your heels ... So be a good chap and gallop up here — at the double!"

Despite my suggested need for urgency, several minutes elapsed before there came a discreet knock on the door and a voice saying: "Courtney Fisk here, sir. The manager!"

He was a dapper little fellow that I let into the room. The pencil-thin moustache and perfectly parted hair, in a style reminiscent of the nineteen-thirties, was at variance with the extrovert line of tweeds he was wearing. Somehow he seemed to lack the style and sartorial perfection that I had come to expect from hotel managers. Although, in fairness, I'm only too aware that it takes all sorts . . .

"It *really* is all that important, sir?" he queried somewhat superciliously, gazing up at me from where his block-heeled shoes only managed to raise him to a bare five-feet-three inches.

"The former occupant of this room . . . when did she book in?" I asked.

"The *gentleman* who last enjoyed a brief sojourn with us in room 12A — and it *was* a gentleman, not a lady — checked out about ten days ago . . . a sales representative for one of the larger agricultural machinery firms. A regular visitor with us, I might add."

"There's been no one else assigned to this room since then?"

"Definitely not." And then no doubt fearing that his words be misconstrued as a disloyalty to the Hotel Bellevue, he added, "It's a week or so before the full holiday season commences. By the end of this month we'll be booked to the eaves."

Not if my recent discovery in the bathroom reached the ears of some of the tourists and holiday-makers who normally take delight in exploring the Cotswolds, I thought. Of course, there are always a few ghouls who would seek out anything as sensational as a murder — but not your average run of folk, thank goodness!

"Then, did a blonde young lady ever accompany your last visitor, or stay with him here?" I queried.

Courtney Fisk's eyebrows lifted like a

pair of startled caterpillars. "Absolutely not, sir. I know there are so-called modern establishments that regrettably countenance such — er — clandestine arrangements, but this hotel — never!"

Silently wondering whether this lack of appreciation for untrammelled love might not be the reason for the hotel's lack of clientele in this flaming June month of roses and unbridled passion, I asked whether he had misplaced any blonde members of his staff. Perhaps the odd chamber-maid wasn't doing her duty by checking on all her chambers.

"We have no young members of your description on my staff," the manager rejoined, a trifle huffily.

"In that case, perhaps you had better venture into the bathroom, here."

"But I assure you, sir, that every room in this hotel is *scrupulously* cleaned before each new arrival."

"Not this one. I could never take a bath in there, the way the place has been left," I assured him. "Could you? Please check, because someone's been a mite careless with their litter, as I think you'll have to agree."

"Oh, if you insist, sir. I still have to finalise dining-arrangements downstairs," he grumbled, as he vanished into the inner cubicle.

It was a markedly disorientated character who tottered out to rejoin me a few seconds — a very few seconds — later.

"How long has Miss — Miss Quinton — been there like that?" he gulped.

"Would you care to make a guess, old son? Understand that she was already installed when I arrived . . . and offhand I'd say that it's most important that you do understand that — and so inform the fuzz!"

"Oh, what's to be done? Such a scandal for the Bellevue! Whatever shall we do?"

"Less of the 'we' if you don't mind," I gently chided. "*You* should call the police . . . but you can leave me right out of it. I expected a non-tenanted room. I've heard of double-booking with some of you hotel-types, but this, if I may say so, is bloody ridiculous!"

Characters in old-style novels were said to wring their hands. Now I witnessed fiction becoming fact as the hotel manager abandoned himself to a display of manual emotion. Poor old Courtney's fingers writhed together like the well-manicured but tormented tentacles of a pair of baby squids.

"What will Judge Quinton say?" he finally moaned.

"Who's Judge Quinton? A relative of the dead girl?"

"Her father — and a right terror he is!" Courtney had quickly lost his upper-class accent. "The old boy owns a large mansion here in Chilworth — across the valley there," he jerked an indicative thumb in the general direction of the window. "They say that if he had his way he'd still arrange for poachers to be transported to Botany Bay — or have 'em topped at the scene of their crime."

"Sounds like an extremely socially

conscious gentleman," I murmured. "Tell me, how is he with the general run of drug trafficking?"

The little manager's eyes went blank and I could see that he had failed to comprehend. I repeated the question.

"Drug trafficking . . . " he mouthed the words after me. "Whatever gives you the idea that Miss Quinton was involved with drugs?"

"I'm not saying that she was. I just wondered how the Judge feels about such a decadent social matter."

"The old boy belongs to some way-out religious group, I understand. When he's on the bench, any criminal, no matter what, can expect to be put away for the maximum sentence that he can dole out, but I've heard it said that he goes absolutely bananas when anyone's found guilty of handling drugs."

'I've an idea that this justice-gentleman is due for something of a double shock,' I thought. To the overwrought Courtney Fisk I said, "Better inform the police without any further delay." I glanced at my watch. "When I'm questioned by the police, as I'm bound to be, I will have to tell them that I reported the murdered girl's presence at 11.47 a.m. on June the 13th. So look slippy, I've no doubt they'll want every minute accounted for."

"Of course! Of *course!*" He glanced at the telephone on the bedside cabinet. "I would rather this didn't go through the switchboard. I'll call the police from my direct outside line in the office downstairs. Would you stay here with the door locked until the law comes? It simply wouldn't do for any of the other guests, or even the staff to know what's happened."

"I think you're being a mite too secretive," I told him. "Everyone will know soon enough. But I'll keep guard for you. Just tell the cops to get a move on."

The little manager scurried from the room. His last anguished words: "Oh, why did it have to be Mr. Justice

Quinton's step-daughter?" were like a verbal sword of Damocles to mark his distressed departure.

★ ★ ★

I suppose it's some seven or eight miles, as the crow flies, from Chilworth to where the main body of the local Law is stationed. Without engaging in any actual flying the fuzz exceeded my expectations. The Hotel Bellevue had been well-named. Perched on a fairly high ridge to the west of the valley, it offered me a fine view of the surrounding countryside from my room window. Within an astoundingly short space of time I could make out two police-cars speeding along the narrow lane which culminated at the Bellevue. They had either sped along the White Way or branched off the A429 to come through Calmsden and Pinkwell. But no matter which direction they had taken, speed limits must have been grossly ignored. Would mention of the Judge's name have provided the incentive for such alacrity?

As they drew closer, the cars showed up intermittently through the screening beech-leaves outside my window. They disappeared from view for a moment as they entered the narrowing road that cut beneath the old viaduct of the disused railway line. When they reappeared they were speeding up the sharp incline leading to the hotel forecourt. Here, they braked sharply. Several uniformed figures and two civilians alighted from the vehicles and crunched their purposeful way across the chipped limestone drive to the hotel entrance.

I hadn't long to remain alone on guard in Room 12A. Obedient to a single sharp knock, I swung the door open and was confronted by a square, solid block of a man. I just knew that this wasn't the gas-man to check the meter.

"Inspector Marlow," he introduced himself brusquely as he shouldered his way into the room. "The Manager reckons you've something to show me."

I took quick stock of the man. Ruddy-faced; grey-blue eyes slightly bagged with age or disillusionment; luxuriant, grizzled eyebrows set apart above a pugnacious nose and mouth; a thick body that had not completely traded in its muscle for the softness of an easier middle-aged way of life; the whole giving him the look of a local farmer of solid yeoman forebears rather than a ranking member of the fuzz. Indeed, as I subsequently learned, he originated from a well-heeled Cotswold farming family who had mis-directed himself into the police-force in his youth and was now only awaiting retirement in a couple of years' time before returning to the land.

"Well, don't just stand there, man. Where is the dead girl?"

"Here, in the bath, Inspector." I pushed open the bathroom door and stood obsequiously aside to allow him the full width of the doorway for his entrance.

He withdrew within a few minutes and gave me the benefit of an icily piercing stare from those hard eyes. "Have a look at her, Doc," he said to a civilain type of a slightly foreign but distinguished-looking order who was a member of that small entourage which I now saw had been waiting discreetly in the corridor outside. "Careful what you touch!"

Some ten minutes elapsed before the dapper doctor reappeared, drying his well-manicured hands on a hotel towel. "She was probably alive some four or five hours ago," he said. "Can be more more precise after a thorough examination, of course."

"Drowned?" demanded the Inspector.

The medico shrugged. "Not necessarily so. The only signs of external injury is a bruising at the throat. She could have been strangled then placed in the bath. She could even have died from natural causes. Any attempt at strangulation may not have been sufficient to extinguish life."

"Hmph! Normal causes!" grunted Inspector Marlow, incredulously. "I can sense nothing normal about Miss Quinton's death. She was your patient, wasn't she, Doc? Did you know that she was injecting herself?"

"I haven't seen the young lady for well over a year now," replied the doctor rather frostily. "At that trime, to my knowledge, there was no call for medication of any sort whatsoever."

"Her left forearm was like a ruddy badly-healed pin-cushion," I heard the Inspector mumble to himself. "All right, you lot," he turned to the remainder of his followers. "You know the drill: photographs, measurements, prints — and don't gambol about the place like a herd of bloody elephants and fudge up any evidence."

"Excuse me, sir, will you be interviewing the hotel staff here or back at the Station?" asked a young sergeant, who to my jaundiced eye didn't look old enough to have need for a razor on those peach-smooth cheeks, despite the silky, incipent moustache that he was trying to encourage to ornament his upper lip. They do say that when the police begin to look frightfully young then you must be getting frightfully old. So be it! Right at that moment I felt at least aged enough to be the young sergeant's father. I could only hope that his mother wasn't an old girl-friend!

"I'll see the lot of 'em here, to begin with. Might have to encourage one or two of them to accompany us back to the Station, after that," said his superior.

Being a sensitive soul, I didn't like the look he gave me, with those final words.

"Shall I take notes for you, or would you like W.P.C. Clarke, here to sit in on the interviews? Her shorthand's better than mine," said the sergeant, with an ingratiating smirk in the direction of the amply-developed young woman police constable who was a member of the entourage.

Inspector Marlow cast a censorious glance in the direction of the aforementioned, uniformed young lady, who was simpering sweetly at the young sergeant, and then with all the natural bonhomie of your died-in-the-wool chauvinistic pig said, "I'll have you to take the notes, sergeant. At least you usually have your mind on the job in hand . . . And now, Mr. Fiske, isn't it?" he turned to the Manager who had contrived to squeeze himself into an unobtrusive corner just inside the door. "I shall need a room to be made available within the next few minutes. I'll be questioning *all* the staff — all of them, mind you. If any of 'em aren't on the premises at the moment, arrange for them to be back here — at the double — or else have a ruddy good excuse ready for any delay in returning . . . I'll also be questioning you, Mister Fisk and this, this gentleman, here." With which he turned and eyed my bearded countenance with a look in which suspicion and dislike were judiciously blended.

★ ★ ★

The Hotel Manager opened up one of the vacant ground-floor rooms for the Inspector's use, and I was given the privilege of initiating the proceedings. It was the young sergeant who ushered me into the inquisition chamber. Of the Inspector there was as yet no sign. While the sergeant busied himself, arranging table and chairs to his satisfaction, I positioned myself in front of a rather good reproduction of Constable's 'The Cornfield' and studied this familiar picture with more care than I had ever previously given it.

A shaft of sunlight brought the print to life — for all the world as though one was looking at the scene through an open window — heightening detail that had never caught my attention before. The picture made me forget for a moment the tragedy of the young blonde, and my main reason for being present in this particular part of the country. I was idly wondering what John Constable would have made of the Cotswolds — how well he would have been able to capture its glory throughout the seasons of the year — when Inspector Marlow heralded his approach with the characteristic half-grunt and half bronchial-explosion which was a preliminary to much of his speech.

"Hmph! Are we all ready then, sergeant?" he asked, and as his minion both nodded and voiced affirmatively, he seated himself behind the table. The inquisition was about to commence!

"Should we inform the next-of-kin, sir?" the sergeant asked.

"I've been trying to do just that," he said, using a tone of voice normally reserved by infant school teachers. "Mr. Justice Quinton has a protracted hearing at the Old Bailey — I'm sure a message will be given him — I have also phoned his home at Chilwell Court. So you see, sergeant, even obvious details have been attended to," he ended sarcastically. "And now, Mr. O'Hara, your Christian names, please."

"Only one forename, Inspector — Michael. The old folks were already rearing such a large brood that when it came to their youngest son they were running out of names, I guess."

"Hmph! Are you Irish?" And this asked as though he expected to see the letters IRA tattooed on my forehead.

"Yes and no, Inspector. Actually, I'm one of those extremely rare birds, a true Britisher. You see I have an ancestry that can boast of Irish, Scots, Welsh and English blood, and, if gossip hasn't been unduly unkind to a maternal great-grandmother, there's probably more than a dash of Danish blood, on the wrong side of the blanket, you understand. That's undoubtedly the reason for my handsome Viking looks!"

"O'Hara, cut out the comedy. You would do well to concentrate on the seriousness of these proceedings. Here, I should say we have an obvious case of murder, and may I point out that you were the first person involved."

"Wouldn't the unfortunate young lady and her assailant, or assailants, be the first involved?" I countered chirpily.

Inspector Marlow glared at me with eyes of sufficient frost to have projected twin icicles in my direction, and then turned a similar stare towards his sergeant who had failed to mask a reprehensible snigger with a contrived cough.

"Have you ever seen the dead girl before?" he continued.

"Never."

"Absolutely certain?" This heavy with suspicion.

"Quite sure. I'd remember a girl like that."

"And why are you here in Chilworth? You've only just booked in, I understand."

"I took the room about an hour ago. I'm here partly on holiday and partly on business."

"Most convenient," said the Inspector heavily. "How do you divide your time?"

"Oh, a little of each, business and pleasure."

"What business would that be? We'll forget the pleasure for the moment," he said, looking at me with the sombre mien of one who obviously suspected me of journeying to the Cotswolds solely for the pleasure of seducing milkmaids in the cowshed.

"Agricultural machinery — hiring out rather than selling — a new line for me." I refrained from mentioning that it was so new that I had only just thought of it.

Thereafter, I found his questions repetitious, always trying to catch me out, but uncompromisingly searching. There was an occasion during the interview when I was in two minds about letting him know my real reason for being present in this neck of the woods, but I eventually decided against breaking my cover, even to a ranking member of the fuzz. Perforce, I had to bend the truth from time to time. His frequent explosive grunts made me well aware that he was far from convinced by my mendacious responses.

His protracted questioning took us well into my normal lunch-time. Was he trying to starve me into submission? But flippancy has its uses. Reluctant as he was to let me go, for he would have dearly loved to corner me into some sort of confession, my more inane replies were causing the Inspector some warmth under the collar. Another ill-repressed snigger from the note-taking sergeant who had been patiently beavering away in a corner of the room, proved the last straw for his superior.

"I'm far from satisfied, Mr. O'Hara, not satisfied at all," he finally snorted, giving me the icy glare from under those rampant brows. "But there are others to see. Hold yourself in readiness for further questioning, possibly back at the station. Don't make any plans for leaving Chilworth for the time being," he ended significantly.

"Wouldn't dream of it, Inspector. I'm here on holiday as well as business, remember. I can't think when last I spent such an interesting morning."

"Conduct yourself in the manner that you've adopted this morning, when you appear in court, and you'll have to take note of such transgressions as contempt and perjury."

"Me, appear in court, Inspector?"

"Innocent or guilty, you'll be appearing in court, Mr. O'Hara." His firm lips then clamped tightly together as though stifling words best left unsaid. A knock on the door drew his attention away from me. "Come, if it's important!" he growled, uninvitingly.

The door to the inquisition room and my mouth opened simultaneously. Framed in the doorway was the blonde whom I had last seen *au naturel* lying in my bath. True, she was now clothed in a most snappy fashion, but I would know that face anywhere!

Startled, I turned to see how the Inspector was taking this apparently miraculous resurrection.

"Hallo, Miss Quinton," he said soberly, rising to his feet. "I'm so sorry that it had to be you! All right, O'Hara, on your way, for now."

2

"I SAID, that will be all, for now, Mr. O'Hara!" The Inspector repeated his dismissal as the blonde visitor entered the room.

Now it so happened that on my way out, and I swear not intentionally, I gently bumped into her. She was alive, all right. And for all I knew kicking, as well! In fact she was a living, breathing doll. Not that there was anything artificial or robot-like about her. I felt sure that no man-made puppet could simulate the heartening movement of those rounded young haunches as she moved gracefully across to where Inspector Marlow was offering her a chair.

It was a further glare from the Chief Inquisitor that finalized my departure. I just caught his next few words, however. They explained a great deal and helped to restore some measure of my mental stability.

"I'm so sorry that you were the one I had to break the sad news to, Miss Judy. Your father will, I expect, have already been told of your sister's death, although I am not certain what provision can be made for him to step down at the Old Bailey. But I've no doubt, in view of this personal tragedy, something will be worked out quite quickly."

So that was it, I thought, closing the door quietly behind me. The dead girl was this blonde's sister. Courtney Fisk whom I met having a near nervous breakdown in the corridor outside — he was next for the inquisition — offered further enlightenment.

"Miss Judy Quinton is Janet's older sister. Janet's the one you found in the bath," he explained.

"Are they identical twins?"

"Strangely, no, in view of the girls' remarkable resemblance to each other. Miss Judy must be at least three years older than her sister."

"Look here, Courtney, I can see that you've been lined up for the next spot of questioning," I said in my most sympathetic tone. "Are you quite sure that you were surprised at seeing this Janet Quinton in the hotel? I can readily appreciate that it was a shock seeing her the way she was, but did she never visit here?"

The dapper little Manager coughed nervously and looked everywhere except at me. "We-ell, she had been here before," he grudgingly admitted. "After all, we're the only licensed premises of any note in Chilworth. There's the pub, 'The Pig and Parsnip' here in Upper Chilworth and a small, rather tatty hotel down in the valley."

"Did she visit often?" I persisted.

"Mm, yes, fairly frequently, I suppose."

"To meet someone here, or was she escorted?" I ploughed on, aware that the Inspector could hold a copyright on these questions.

"She was very friendly with a young man who serves in our bar ... and then there is the gentleman who drives up here from London most weekends. In the beginning he would actually stay in the hotel while looking at property in the district. He's now buying a swish old place between here and Withington. At least, it will be quite a luxurious residence, I hear, when he has it fixed to his liking."

"And Janet Quinton used to meet him here?"

"They would often meet here for a meal, and then they'd go off together, presumably to this new place of his, since Janet Quinton had something of a reputation as an interior designer, particularly for Cotswold houses."

"This place was a valuable property?"

Courtney nodded vigorously. "A cross between a mansion and an extremely large farmhouse, formerly owned by the Yellands — a particularly well-heeled family. Mind you, although Miss Janet may have been advising him about the interior decoration, it hasn't brought much employment to the district. The owner has a team of men working there, for the main part I believe they are housed in the many outbuildings. They're not locals, though, apart from Bill Spriggs the thatcher, over from Fossebridge way. In fact, they're all foreigners. Somehow it doesn't seem right to have them handling Cotswold stonework."

"You mean they really are foreigners?"

"That's right. Most of them are proper Mediterranean types. Two of them could be Londoners — and then there's that ox of an Australian chauffeur . . ."

"And has this landed gentleman a name?" I asked.

"Yes, James Luckin, quite a pleasant, generously spending gentleman with the staff. Always extremely well-groomed. Drives a Rolls 'Corniche', or rather his chauffeur drives him . . . but why so many questions, Mr. O'Hara?"

"Idle curiousity, Courtney, old son.

It's a failing that we O'Haras have had to fight against down through the ages," I said, at the same time wondering just what 'Lucky Jimmy', or James Luckin, esquire, was up to in this little rustic paradise. True, I had never actually met this vice-boss, who'd started as a Soho pimp before scrabbling up the dung-heap to an evil eminence at the top, but I knew a great deal about him. None of it good.

It was at that moment that Judy Quinton was ushered from the interrogation room by Inspector Marlow, who after a warm hand-clasp for the girl, signalled Courtney Fisk, with an imperative nod of his head, that it was the Manager's turn for the verbal rack. Miss Quinton and I were thus left alone, facing each other in the corridor. On closer acquaintance I noticed that although she bore an uncanny resemblance to her dead sister, she looked to have a markedly stronger character in the set of mouth and chin, and most certainly those three extra years of maturity had brought a fullness to her figure, a fullness where it mattered most.

"I'm afraid that I was the one who discovered your sister in such unfortunate circumstances, Miss Quinton," I said.

Blue-grey eyes, shadowed by grief, gave me a long searching look. "You found Janet?"

"Yes. I had just booked into the hotel. Went to the bathroom. There she was."

"Did you know Janet?"

"No. Although I'm not sure that the Inspector is willing to believe that. But, honestly, until I saw your sister in that — that bath — I had never set eyes on her before."

"It's a pity that you had to choose this hotel and were given that room, then."

"I'm afraid so. As I told the Inspector, I'm here in part for a holiday as well as business purposes. So far as this Hotel is concerned, well, beggars can't be choosers, and all that.

This isn't my first visit to Chilworth. Normally I rent a cottage off a widowed lady in the village. I was pipped on the post, however. The cottage has already been let to some early holiday-makers and won't be available for another week or so."

A faint smile wiped some of the grief from those fine eyes. "Don't worry too much — Mr. O'Hara, isn't it? If you're innocent you've nothing to fear from Bob Marlow. He may be very gruff in the course of duty, but he's a fair man. And since he's a friend of the family, my sister's death has probably hit him as hard as any of us."

As she made to move away, I suddenly realised that I didn't want this acquaintanceship to end in such a summary fashion. "Would you — care to lunch with me, here at the hotel?" I asked tentatively, knowing full well that this was not the time nor the place to try to date this girl.

She shook her head of close-cropped blonde hair. "Thanks. No. I really don't feel like a meal, at the moment."

"That's understandable in the circumstances. Perhaps coffee or a drink?" I persisted like an insensitive loon.

"Sorry. Some other time, perhaps. I must return home now in case there's a message coming through from my father in London."

"A lift home? My car's just outside."

"So is my car. So, no thank you, again." This last with a final, negative shake of that adorable blonde head before she continued on her way towards the hotel entrance.

Some minutes later, from a window flanking my seat in the Hotel dining-room, I watched her having a few words with the police-doctor, before she climbed elegantly into a 1.8 orange Marina and headed off down the drive. There was no doubt about it, the O'Hara charm had singularly failed to deliver.

"She's a real nice lass, that one," said the rosy-cheeked, silver-haired waitress who had just reached my table and broke into my thoughts as she noted the direction of my gaze.

"She is all that!" I could only enthusiastically agree.

"It's a terrible thing that's happened to her sister. I'll wager that the old Judge will be bringing some heavy pressure to bear on those in authority round here. He'll not rest until whoever's responsible for that poor girl's death is caught and punished. And he won't let anyone else round here rest, if I know anything about him."

"Judge Quinton is a hard man, I hear."

"There are some who would think so, especially muggers and other violent crooks, as well as anyone connected with selling drugs to young people, who've been sentenced by him in court. For my money they've deserved all they've got. Now that Janet, his youngest and favourite step-daughter has been found murdered there'll be hell to pay. Take my word for it," she paused. "There, as usual I'm talking too much. Would you care to order lunch now, sir?"

"A ham-salad with roll and butter, followed by Cotswold cheese and biscuits, will do just fine," I said.

"Plain Cotswold cheese, sir, or the one with onions and chives?"

"I'm not likely to be kissing anyone today. Let's make it the Cotswold cheese with added onions and chives — and a carafe of white wine, please."

With a smile that creased the corners of her eyes, she moved off to see to my lunch, while I sat back thinking of Judy Quinton, and what a pity it was that I had no need to abstain from the onions and chives. Now if she had realised that today was my birthday, would that have made any difference to my choice of cheese?

A while later, having served me, the waitress lingered conversationally, for there remained only two other diners in the room and they were at the cigarettes and coffee stage.

"Has the Judge any other children?" I asked, cutting into a generously thick slice of prime ham to reduce it to more masticatory proportions.

"There's an older son from his first marriage. I've never seen him. He's rumoured to be something of a black sheep. He eventually went out East as a plantation manager I believe. A very clever young man, though. Supposed to have university degrees in this and that."

I grinned to myself. They were offering degrees in the oddest subjects, these days. "So, just the one son and two step-daughters from a second marriage. How come the daughters have the same surname?" I asked, round a portion of thickly buttered fresh bread-roll.

"It's quite a romantic story. His first wife, poor thing, suffered some sort of a nervous breakdown and then seemed to go rapidly downhill so far as her health was concerned. Within eighteen months of his wife's death, the Judge married a widow of one of his Army friends. He served in Burma, fighting against the Japs. He was a Brigadier, you know," she said this with pride. "His friend is said to have saved his life when their headquarters was over-run by the Japs. Both men survived the war, although his friend, name of Major Strickland, I believe, had to have an arm amputated. This didn't stop him setting up an antique shop in Stow-on-the-Wold, nor from fathering two daughters. Well, cutting it short, when the Major died, Judge Quinton married Mrs. Strickland, a really handsome woman, a mite younger than the Judge, of course, and it was decided that the two girls, Janet and Judy should have their names changed to Quinton."

"Why was it that Miss Quinton was first up here to see the Inspector? Is the mother in London with the Judge?"

"The Judge's second wife has been dead for several years now. A riding accident. Although he's reputed to be a hard man, he grieved sorely over the loss of that woman, I can tell you. The family have had more than their share of tragedy. And now the youngest girl found dead like this — the Judge really cherised young Janet." She paused and we both looked out of the window as there came the scrunch of tyres on the drive and an ambulance drove up to the hotel entrance.

"They've come to take the poor lass away, I suppose. Will there be a 'topsy, d'you think?"

"Yes. A violent death like that will need full medical investigation."

The old waitress tut-tutted softly to herself. "She was a wayward young thing in some ways, but many of the youngsters are, these days. She was easily led, I'd say, and not always in the right direction. Not a bit like her sister, Judy, who's a really sound girl. Although on looks alone it was sometimes hard to tell them apart."

"Have you been interviewed by Inspector Marlow?" I asked. "If not, your turn will come, you know."

She dimpled apple-rosy cheeks. "Bobby Marlow will have to watch his step with me," she confided. "We were teenagers together. Our families were neighbours when we lived at Bourton-on-Water. If his memory is still as good as mine, seeing me again may well bring a twinkle back into those blue eyes of his. My, but when he was a young man he was what today's youngsters call real 'dishy'." With this, and a twinkle in her own eyes, she retired to the kitchen.

Lunch over, and no immediate call on my time, I decided to take a gentle stroll round this rambling old Cotswold village. As I left the hotel, the ambulance pulled out just ahead of me. It was followed by one of the police cars, bearing away some of the Inspector's merry men, but leaving the head-ranking fuzz and his sergeant still installed at the hotel.

Idly wondering how others of the hotel staff were going to fare in the inquisition-room, I followed the road down under the disused railway viaduct and with homely stone-built cottages flanking me on either side I turned right up a narrow lane that led past the fine late Norman church, standing on high ground overlooking the village. I paused long enough to note the early use of Arabic numerals on the church turret, dated 1465, and fell to wondering just what it must have been like here in the village's heyday, when it had enjoyed the wealth and prestige generated by a prosperous international wool trade.

The lane now levelled out and made for easier walking. Passing the Manor on my right, a finely preserved building that could still boast of some original medieval parts — I turned left at the cross-roads, paused to read the few notices that had been placed on the notice-board here, flushed a brace of young pheasants from the roadside and stood watching as they took wing over some dry-stone walling, skimming low over the field beyond before disappearing from sight in a tangled thicket lower down in the valley.

This sort of gentle stroll was meat and drink to me, and was one reason why I returned to the Cotswolds, year after year. As I walked the sun-dappled lanes I could almost feel my personal batteries busily recharging themselves. Prior to this I had spent a hectic couple of months on the Isle of Guernsey. Not holidaying on that trip, I might add. Even as I walked I could feel the slight, uncomfortable pull of adhesive-plaster, high on my right rib-cage, where a certain uncouth gentleman, having taken an active dislike to Mrs. O'Hara's favourite son, had been extraordinarily careless with his flick-knife.

I passed few people during that stroll round Chilworth, but those I did meet, gave me a pleasant time-of-the-day, as they walked their dogs, tended their front gardens or, like myself, were just out taking the air on this fine June afternoon.

Before tackling the gentle climb out of the lower valley, which after three miles or so would lead me back to the hotel, I found myself a grassy slope beneath a beech-tree, lit up a small panatella cigar and sat there listening and watching while the smaller world of nature rustled about its business. An hour passed all too easily. This, I decided, must have been the birthday present I had been promising myself. When I finally came to my size nines again and brushed some wisps of grass from my nether person, I found it rather disconcerting to realize that a confirmed bachelor like myself, who had always sought safety by playing the field, had spent overmuch time with his thoughts centred on a certain Judge's daughter — the live one, of course — whom I had first met that morning.

When I eventually made it back to the hotel, I could scarcely repress a groan at being greeted by Inspector Marlow, seated by himself in one of the most comfortable armchairs in the foyer.

"Hmph! A few more moments of your time," was his greeting as he led me towards his favourite room.

This time we were alone together, with no sign of the sergeant. For a few seconds there was an uncomfortable silence. The Inspector stood with his broad back to the window giving me, in the vernacular, a very old-fashioned look.

"Something worrying you?" I ventured, at last.

"Mister O'Hara," and he really took his time over my name. "I'm quite certain that you have not been as frank with me as I could have wished."

"But I answered all your questions, Inspector — to your satisfaction, I trust," I replied, adopting the air of puzzled innocence of one who has just finished burnishing his halo.

"You had an answer for all my questions," agreed the Inspector, giving me his special, refrigerated look. "But I would have preferred the whole truth, without any dissembling as to the real reason for your presence in this part of the country."

"Would you like to question me again, if anything's worrying you?" I asked, knowing full well that he intended just that.

He began his second round of inquisition casually enough. "Shall we leave any slick evasive answers right out of it? Simple replies will be appreciated. Now, you say that you're here, in part, on holiday. Have you ever stayed at the Bellevue Hotel on other occasions?"

"No, whenever I've been in Chilworth before I've rented a small cottage owned by a widowed lady, Mrs. Martin, a perfectly respectable person."

"Why didn't you rent the cottage this time? And where is it?"

"It's over at Westlea End. Other holiday visitors pipped me with my booking, at least for this week. When they leave I've made arrangements to take over the cottage again. Until then

I propose to remain on here at the hotel."

"Are you planning a protracted stay, then?"

"Possibly three, maybe four weeks — it all rather depends on how the business part of my visit ticks over."

"Hmph! You're no stranger to the Cotswolds?"

"No. I've spent many an enjoyable and peaceful holiday in your part of the country, Inspector. It hasn't always been a summer visit either. Each season has its own charm here. I've even been snowed up in the cottage I mentioned, with all power and telephone lines down for three or four days. But with plenty of food in the pantry and logs for the fire, plus a clutch of paper-backs on the shelves, I found it quite relaxing."

"Yes, we do get some pretty severe weather, at times," he admitted, seeming to mellow slightly. "Have you always stayed here in Chilworth? We have other attractive places y'know."

"Down through the years I've holidayed in other towns and villages, most of them in Gloucestershire. I've spent interesting and happy enough times in Cirencester, Stow-on-the-Wold, Tetbury, Bourton-on-Water, Lower Slaughter — there's a perfect picture-book village — and so on."

Moving from his position in front of the window, the Inspector used several silent moments ramming tobacco into the bowl of a well-cured briar, seated his bulk on a corner of the table, which made a creaking protest at this liberty, and then having spent two Swan Vestas before he had his pipe ignited to his satisfaction, eyed me complacently through a haze of blue smoke.

"Why is it always the Cotswolds? Any strong family connections with us?" he asked.

"No connections. I came here simply because I like this part of the country. Much of my time takes me to cities. They're all right for shopping, theatres, and what have you, but I'm not over the moon about crowded cities, nor equally crowded coastal resorts. Gloucestershire is only a couple of hours run out on the M4 from London, and it offers the quiet, relaxing country atmosphere that I enjoy."

"I shouldn't think you've enjoyed it quite so much, this time, Mr. O'Hara," he said, removing his pipe from between well-maintained but slightly irregular incisors and inspecting its stem with an interest that it hardly warranted.

"I'll admit that it's the first holiday that I've been greeted with a corpse on my arrival. A charming enough one, I grant you. In fact, rather a waste of good material. But a corpse, none the less."

"You'll know of course, by now, that the dead girl is Janet Quinton — Mr. Justice Quinton's daughter. If you haven't found out from other sources, Millie Gray will no doubt have told you."

"Millie Gray?" I queried.

"A rather garrulous little waitress," he said amiably. "She mentioned that you were questioning her rather closely about the Quinton family. Since you've visited here before it's surprising that you have never heard of them. True, they keep much to themselves but they do live here you know, on the other side of the valley."

"I may have heard of them before, Inspector, but I can't honestly say that it ever registered in what passes for a memory with me. It was only simple curiosity that prompted me to ask the waitress about them. By the way, Inspector, she told me that you both knew each other — er — quite well in earlier days at Bourton."

"That's undeniable fact," he replied imperturbably. "Millie was talkative even in those days — but not without her attractions . . . But getting back to the Quintons: I assume that you have never met up with the dead girl on previous visits here? She also had her attractions — and rumour has it that she could be quite free with them."

"To my knowledge I've never set eyes on Janet Quinton before today."

"Hmph! Did it register with you that she was injecting herself? It was certainly not on her doctor's orders, or so Doctor Nash assures me. Y'know, I rather fear it may have been some sort of drug . . . dope, you understand? But then, of course you'd understand, since you're a working member of INIT."

'And there goes my cover,' I thought. I wondered how he had found me out?

His rather leathery face creased to a sudden grin. "I saw you about a year ago, at the Yard. You didn't have that beard in those days, but I've an excellent memory for faces. A 'phone call to the right person, a little while ago, soon put me in the picture. Even a humble country cop gets to know a few right persons in the course of time," and he sucked long and satisfyingly at his briar.

"You're right," I admitted. "Actually

I am on leave, but I'm also taking the opportunity to nose around here quietly. A certain gentleman in the 'Scrubs' has squeaked — not much, mind you, but enough to point the finger in this direction. He mentioned something about a Cotswold connection operating from this neck of the woods."

"I see. And since you're a very successful operator with our branch of the International Narcotics Investigation Team it's got to be connected with dope. And in my Manor!" he shook his head sorrowfully. "There's modern crime for you: make your fortune by ruining thousands of kids' lives."

3

BEFORE Inspector Marlow left the hotel he assured me that, so far as he was concerned, my cover was still intact. His telephone call to Scotland Yard had been discreet on an outside line, and no one had been present with him at the time. So we parted on much friendlier terms than had been the case of our first question-and-answer time together. I had come to appreciate his ability and to recognise that while he was a good steady cop who for the most part tried to play it from the book, if and when circumstances demanded it, he would not be averse to slipping in the odd paragraph or two of his own if this ensured that law and order would prevail in his manor.

"Any help I can offer . . . only too pleased . . . Get a quiet message to me whenever you like. Remember we're on the same side . . . In a way it's all too easy to pick up the drug-pusher and the user, the small-time smuggler, and even minor villains who take their orders from the Big Boys. But it is the brains behind these operations that we want to snaffle," had been his parting words. And there had been no doubting his sincerity.

Left to my own devices I settled myself into room number 6 since 12A was now out of bounds to all but the fuzz. I checked on the new bathroom but all was in order. The remainder of the time before dinner I spent rather unprofitably sounding out other members of the hotel staff whom I chanced to meet. Their questioning at the hands of the Inspector had been thorough, but none could throw any light on Janet Quinton's murder. About the only grain of information that I came up with, and I've no doubt that even this hadn't escaped Marlow, was the inference that little Janet had been more than just friends with the mature student type who normally dispensed drinks behind the bar. His name was Gary Warren, and today being his time off he had so far escaped the Inspector's net.

After an early dinner that may not have sent your avowed gastronome into transports of delight, but certainly satisfied me with its plain but wholesome dishes of grilled trout, generously-sliced leg of lamb, a near ninety degree wedge of blackcurrant tart adorned with a hearteningly large dollop of cream, the whole being aided on its trip down the alimentary canal by draughts of a reasonably-priced but quite palatable little house wine, I then decided to take a final stroll on this splendid June evening.

This time, having passed under the old viaduct and sniffed at a faint air of wood-smoke, I took the lower road below the church. As I well knew, this led me to that hospitable old Chilworth inn, *The Pig and Parsnip*, nestling in a hollow opposite an ancient watermill where a small but fast-flowing stream cascaded over worn limestone in a miniature waterfall before flowing away to disappear into a gridded culvert farther down the lane.

Undecided about enjoying a malt-and-water, or two, after such a satisfying meal at the hotel, I had just drawn on the full reserves of the O'Hara willpower and was actually passing the inn on my left when I noticed a Rolls Corniche parked in the forecourt. Dammit all, I reasoned, thereby sending willpower packing, it was still my birthday, and promptly circumnavigated a low stone wall and opened the door of the cosy saloon bar of the pub.

Once inside, it didn't take me long to sort out the owner of the Rolls. Probably well into his forties, a thick body now carrying more than its fair share of flab, strands of greasy black hair brushed economically over a pink scalp, overfull moist lips that told their own story of appetite, and shifty, calculating eyes that didn't seem to miss a trick.

He was standing to one side of the wide stone hearth, his expensively tailored chalk-stripe suit just a little too tightly waisted for true sartorial elegance, his flamboyant silk tie and matching breast-pocket handkerchief, plus handmade light tan leather shoes, all looking oddly out of place here in this snug country inn.

I knew that his sharp eyes had noted my entrance. Apart from my first swift appraisal I studiously avoided looking in his direction, quickly falling into conversation with a bucolic character at the bar who was confiding his marital problems to me after the first five minutes, followed by the more important matter of the trouble besetting his pigs.

Having extricated myself from my talkative companion when he was joined at the bar by one of his regular cronies, I took a second malt whisky and water across to a corner seat. This had recently been vacated by a courting couple and the warmth of their residence still lingered on the leather upholstery. Seated there, weighing up a few personal pros and cons while enjoying my drink and a small cigar, I was intrigued to see a burly, becapped figure in a chauffeur's uniform shoulder his way into the entrance of the saloon and give the owner of the Rolls a curt nod before retiring again in the direction of the public bar. There would appear to be few words wasted between servant and master.

While I was still watching the chauffeur's departure, I was interested to see a flame-coloured Morris Marina park in the forecourt just outside the saloon window and then saw Judy Quinton alight from the vehicle. Being of a suspicious turn of mind it occurred to me that, as we academics so pithily put it, the servant had been giving his master the nod.

Sure enough, upon entering the

saloon, the girl headed for the owner of the Rolls and immediately began a low but obviously animated conversation with him. Because of some leisure-time work with handicapped youngsters — a little sweetener to offset the sourer side of my nature — I have some practice at lip-reading. Whilst I could now neither see nor hear what the girl was saying with scarcely suppressed anger, for she had turned so that only a pleasingly lissom back was presented to me, I still enjoyed a full frontal of her companion. After a minute or two while perforce he had to listen to what was obviously some form of heated censure, his dark eyes hooded, colour suffused the meaty cheeks, and his thick lips writhed out the words:

"You bloody stupid little bitch!"

Judy Quinton's answer to this was a beautiful round-arm swing that brought her right hand into such smart contact with the other's fleshy face as to cause all talk in the room to be immediately silenced. The shocked expression on that over-fed face did my old heart a power of good. But the following glare of sheer murder in his eyes was not so pleasing, nor was his action of swiftly reaching out a plump but powerful beringed paw to grab the girl cruelly by the arm. As I saw her wince to the obvious pain he must be causing, I just knew that it was time for me to make his acquaintance.

"Good evening, Miss Quinton," I said pleasantly. "How nice to see you again so soon. Could I have a quiet word, when you can tear yourself away from your present company?"

Her overdressed companion all but snarled at my intrusion and those satanic eyes slitted as he mentally assessed my physical capabilities. Fortunately — and I've had good reason to be thankful for this many times before — all male members of the O'Hara clan have been blessed with generous thews. I am certain that it was my six feet plus chassis rather than my honest but homely face, only partly obscured by a well-nurtured rufous beard, which caused him, a mite reluctantly 'tis true, to release his grip on the girl's arm.

Without another word I slipped a comforting hand under Judy Quinton's elbow and escorted her from the saloon bar out to where her car was parked. Beneath the powder-blue two-piece that she was wearing I could feel the tremors racking her.

"Nothing to be afraid of now," I murmured.

"I'm *not* afraid . . . I'm just in one hell of a temper!" the forthright young lady assured me. "I'm annoyed with myself and livid with — with other people!"

"Like to talk it out of your system?" I suggested, hopefully.

"It's family stuff . . . rather personal . . ."

"Sorry. Didn't mean to intrude, especially after the shock of your sister's death. But that character in the bar wasn't being too friendly.

Would you like me to go back there and — er — remonstrate with him?"

She moistened her gorgeous lips just before they lifted to a smile. "Thanks for the offer. A minute or so ago I would have taken you up on that — possibly joined in and helped you. But not now. He isn't worth it. How Janet ever had dealings with him I'll never know."

"Oh, that's it. He's a friend of your sister's?"

"The sort of friend she could well have done without, poor girl," and then, anger taking hold again and breaking down her reticence, she added, "do you know, he had the nerve to 'phone me, assuring me that he had something of importance to tell me about Janet and asking me to meet him here tonight."

"And did he have anything of significance to say?"

"Just — just the same obscenities that he was hinting at in his 'phone call," she paused and looked at me searchingly. "Why are some men such — such animals?" she asked.

I shrugged. "Judging by the look of that fellow he could give lessons in it. Even we normal male chauvinists draw the line at his type."

She smiled again, this time with her eyes as well as her lips. About to slide into the driving seat of the Marina, she paused and eyed me thoughtfully. "Are you going straight back into the bar?"

"There is a half-finished whisky . . . "

"Could you possibly forego that pleasure and accompany me on a short drive?"

Could I! Can dogs scratch themselves when they itch? "Of course. Only too pleased," I yapped, hastening round to the passenger's seat before she regretted the impulse. Mind you, I'm not such a dumb cluck. I was well aware that the invitation had been tendered with the sole idea of saving me from running into any trouble with her former companion. But we O'Haras will grab at the smallest of mercies that Providence thrusts our way. Yes,

I know, we're sadly lacking in pride.

"I have an appointment with Doctor Grant near Northleach. You possibly saw him when the police brought him to the Bellevue to attend my sister," she said, easing the Marina from the inn's forecourt, while I adjusted the front passenger seat so that my knees were less of a hazard to my chin. And then, with a smile at my minor contortions, she added, "It's not often that Maud and I have such a long-legged passenger."

"Maud?" I queried.

"Maudie Marina," she offered. "Don't you give your car a name? I always like to be on friendly terms with my current four-wheeled tin box."

"We all have our little quirks," I grinned. "Usually, the only names I've ever used on any of my cars are when they fail to start in the morning, or die out on me at a busy crossroads."

"You should never swear at a car," she admonished. "After all they are considered to be of feminine gender, just like boats, and they can't answer back."

"Not very feminine if they don't answer back. But just for you I'll watch my language in future," I said. "By the way, why the visit to the doc's? Not feeling too well?"

"Oh, I'm quite all right, thanks. Stephen also 'phoned me about Janet."

"Stephen?"

"Doctor Stephen Grant. He's a friend of the family. In fact, at one time we were engaged but very sensibly we broke it off. He's several years older than me and well-steeped in local politics. Mind you, he's no fuddy-duddy," she added loyally, "but his interests just aren't mine. We parted the best of friends."

"So local politics aren't your scene?"

The cheek facing me dimpled slightly. "I'd sooner curl up with a good book."

"Lucky book," I replied, and noted that the dimple deepened splendidly.

We were passing Stowell before she spoke again, and then it was to voice a faint curiosity about my presence in this neck of the woods. Assuring her of the innocence of my visit, we settled down for another quiet but enjoyable drive until we reached the outskirts of Northleach. Doctor Grant's house was a typical Cotswold homestead, built of stone even to the roof tiles. It was much larger than most cottages and the splendidly maintained front garden bespoke either a G.P. with such a small practice that he had time on his hands to indulge in gardening, or else such a rewarding clientele that he was able to afford help with his hallowed plot. It chanced that as we pulled up in the lane outside the cottage, a short, but powerfully-built man was just opening the door of a gleaming bronze 3-litre Capri Ghia. As he turned, I recognised the sleek black hair and sallow complexion. It was Doctor Grant, whom I had last seen from the hotel dining-room window having a few words with Judy.

Directly he saw us, he crossed over

to where we were parked. "I'm sorry about this, Judy," he apologised. "Just had an urgent call from Mrs. Spriggs over Fossebridge way. Her husband took a nasty tumble on a roofing job, late this afternoon. Should have called me earlier, of course, but you know what a tough old son of the soil Bill Spriggs is. He made light of things until he tried to come to his feet after a spell watching T.V. His wife tells me that he's now locked in position in his favourite armchair, and is in some considerable pain."

This was the first chance I'd had of studying the good Doctor at close range. I guessed that he was well into his forties, with just a hint of mixed blood. The dark eyes and sallow cheeks could have owed something to the Mediterranean region, or even east of that.

"Was it anything of importance that you wanted to discuss with me — about Janet?" Judy asked.

The Doctor shot a curious glance

in my direction as though he had only just realized that I was there. My companion noticed the look and hurriedly explained my presence.

"This is — " she paused, suddenly aware that she didn't know my name.

"Michael O'Hara — Mike for short," I obliged.

"Mr. O'Hara has been most protective this evening. He was also the first one to find poor Janet."

"Ah!" Now I had Dr. Grant's full attention. "A most unfortunate business, I'm afraid. The poor girl used to be a patient of mine — is still on my books, I do believe. I wouldn't have thought she had an enemy in the world."

"She appeared to have been using a hypodermic on herself," I ventured.

"I know nothing about that. So far as I am aware there was no medical reason why she should have been administering to herself," he replied, thoughtfully. "Could she have been taking drugs, do you think, Judy?"

"I've no idea. She used to run around with some weirdos, drop-out types who were all set to change the establishment. But I've never thought there was any real harm in Janet," she replied. "Once or twice I've mentioned late nights to her — or rather, early mornings — and also about a growing preference for alcohol rather than food ... But as for drugs — I can't believe it."

The Doc. was worried, I could see. That fine forehead creased to a frown. "I must get myself across to Spriggs' place, but I'll be in touch again. Perhaps we could have another word at some time, Mr. O'Hara?"

"Any time. I'm a free agent, on holiday for a couple of weeks or so," I said.

"Thanks. Sorry to have dragged you over here, Judy ... and I'm so dreadfully sorry about your sister."

Together, we watched as he swung the Capri out into the lane behind us and zoomed off into the gathering dusk. That showy little flivver had more power under its bonnet than was necessary for some of these narrow Cotswold lanes.

I looked across at Judy and saw grief suddenly shadow her eyes. "When you found my sister, was there nothing — absolutely nothing that could provide a clue as to her attacker?"

"Not a thing. I did search the place before the police arrived. But without result."

"And you say that Janet had marks on her arm . . . ?"

I saw no reason in lying. "I'm afraid so. I'm quite certain that she had been injecting herself."

A low sob escaped her and one hand went up to mask her eyes. "Would you mind taking over the driving?" she said, at last. "At least as far as the Hotel. It's as though I've only just begun to realize that my kid sister, always the life and soul of the party, isn't with us any longer."

"It would be a pleasure," I said, and

with a comforting hand to her shoulder helped her round to the passenger seat.

I had been driving for several minutes before she regained something of her composure. Happening to glance her way I saw her eyeing me in a speculative manner.

"You try to pretend that you're awfully tough, don't you?" she observed.

"D'you think so?" I asked casually, being well aware that in my time over the past five or six years I had been forced to be tougher than she could have ever imagined.

She suddenly smiled in that heart-warming manner. "Of course, your looks help you a lot in that deception."

It was my nose, I felt sure. My beard drew some attention away from it, but there is no doubt that several pro fights in the ring, plus the odd game of rugger, had left the old proboscis slightly more thickened across the bridge than my parents' genes had intended.

"What really is your job?" she

continued. "And don't give me that line again about starting up a farm-machinery business. I'm not certain that you could tell a combine harvester from a plough."

"You do me an injustice," I said. "Anyway, as I've told you, I'm also here in part on holiday."

"Sorry, I'm not sure that rings true ... Are you — police?"

A Z-bend just coming up kept my eyes to the road, so I answered with a negative shake of the noodle.

"Then, a private eye, perhaps?"

"There's nothing like that about me," I grinned. "I've always looked like this. Would you like to take it up with my mother some time?"

"Do you ever give a straight answer?"

"Only when I'm really cornered ... Now, for a change of subject, how about me dropping you home? I can make my own way back to the Hotel. It's a fine night and I'd enjoy the walk."

"I'll not argue about that," she

agreed. "Thanks."

For the rest of the journey, apart from the odd word or two of direction, she was very quiet. Finally, just outside Upper Chilworth, we arrived at an imposing double-fronted mini-manor and took the lengthy drive that led to the front portals.

"Would you like a coffee?" she asked, "Or since you're walking back, perhaps something a little stronger?"

"Coffee will do fine," I assured her, and followed her into the house.

"Care to come through to the kitchen?" she asked. "An elderly lady from the village helps us out, but there's no one here, at the moment. My step-father hasn't yet had time to return from London, although he's on his way, I understand."

"There's rather a lot of house to be alone in," I said, following her as she switched on various lights as we made our way to the rear of the building. I also felt like adding that there were a great number of tempting goodies in the way of antiques and original paintings to attract the attentions of many a house-breaking, fly-by-night villain. There was no doubt that if the decor and furnishings of his home were anything to go by, Judge Quinton was more than ordinarily well-heeled.

"I've no fear of loneliness," she replied. "In fact, when it's a matter of quietly sorting oneself out, it can be an asset to have just one's own company to answer to."

"You're a strange girl," I said, thinking that there was something amiss with the local swains if someone as attractive as Judy was allowed too much time to be by herself.

I was nose-deep into my second cup of coffee, with Judy still sipping at her first, when the 'phone rang. It was too late for your average social call. The old sixth-sense immediately caused me to think Trouble — complete with a capital T.

"Shall I get it for you, Judy?" I asked, closest to the telephone and already out of my seat.

"Please."

Directly I heard Inspector Marlow's fruity voice I knew I'd been right about trouble, although for whom I couldn't be certain until I had allowed the full import of the Inspector's message to sink in.

"So you've already found your way there, have you, O'Hara? Does grass ever have a chance where you're standing? Can I talk to Miss Quinton?"

"She's here, just finishing a cup of coffee." I know how suspicious some cops are about late-night twosomes. "Can I give her the message?"

"All right. Ask her if the name, Gary Warren, means anything to her?"

"Do you happen to know a Gary Warren?" I duly asked my companion, suddenly realizing that this was the student-type bartender with whom Janet Quinton was reputed to have been on more than speaking terms.

"Yes, he works at the Hotel Bellevue. My sister used to be quite friendly with him. Occasionally, he'd visit us here. Usually when my step-father wasn't around though."

I relayed this information to the Inspector.

"Hmph! He was a friend of the dead girl," agreed Marlow. "Now it's all in the past tense for him as well. He's dead now, himself . . . and rather messily dead, at that!"

4

"**G**ARY WARREN — dead! You mean he's been murdered?"

"It looks that way," agreed the Inspector.

"Where? Here in Chilworth? Not in another bath at the Bellevue, surely?"

"No, his body was found under a hedge by the side of the A443, between Barnsley and Bibury ... Not a pretty sight, I might add. Someone had blasted him at close range with both barrels of a shot-gun. Death must have been instantaneous — but very messy!" The Inspector paused for a moment. "Careful how you break the news to Judy," he added.

It was too late. She had overhead my side of the conversation. "Not Gary Warren, as well," she whispered in a shocked voice. "Can — can there be any connection between his death and my sister's murder?"

I put this same question to Marlow but he was non-committal in reply. He also read more into my words than I had meant to reveal.

"There's no evidence to suggest that Warren killed Janet Quinton and then took his own life, if that's what you have in mind. Indeed, judging by the full frontal blast of what I'd say was a very heavy shotgun, and the absence of any weapon, I should say the odds are against suicide. But there you are. That's all I know at the moment ... By the way, sorry to spoil your social evening."

Replacing the receiver I turned to offer Judy a few comforting words, but she had regained her composure. Lifting her cup she sipped thoughtfully at her coffee.

"Surely there must be some connection, Michael? Here we have two murders in a matter of hours and it must be years and years since last we had such violent deaths in Chilford."

I shrugged. "It certainly seems odd and I grant you that this little village is receiving more than its fair share of skulduggery just now. Are you quite sure you'll not be nervous staying in this house by yourself tonight?" I ventured.

A smile curved her lips. "Is that chivalry or chauvinism speaking?"

"Oh, chivalry every time. We O'Hara's are noted for it."

"I've no doubt," she said. "Just as we Quintons — at least some of us — are noted for our firm use of the negative — in certain situations. So, I'm sorry, Michael, but it's you for the Bellevue. In fact, now that you've finished your coffee I really think it's time we parted. It's quite a step back to the Hotel."

"Hey, that was an offer of pure friendship, with no strings attached!" I said. "I shall worry about you now."

"I'll lock all the doors and windows," she promised, ushering me to the front door.

"There was that creep who arranged a

meeting with you at the *Pig and Parsnip* . . . Supposing he comes knocking?"

"Oh, that awful character. He'll not come around."

"What was he really trying on?"

"Blackmail," Judy said shortly. "He told me that he had pornographic pictures of Janet and Gary together."

"What was his price?"

"Not money. It was a — a service."

"Of a rather intimate nature?"

She nodded.

"That would be when you landed that beautiful right-hand swing?"

"Yes. I don't know whether he has any photographs. I wouldn't like to believe it of Janet. But she was almost a stranger for the last few weeks before she was killed. It was as though all the feckless side of her nature had triumphed over the good . . . Oh, I really miss her, Michael — I really do."

Determined to look into the matter if 'Lucky Jimmy' was still around, I took my leave of Judy and crunched up the moonlit drive towards the road. A glance at my wristwatch revealed that we were just entering the first hour of another day. This year's birthday was over. Ah, well, we all get older by the minute! As I trod the winding shadowy highway that led back to the Bellevue, I fell to wondering how old Judy was. At a guess I'd say she was either a well-preserved twenty-five or a mature twenty-three years. In any event, the age-gap was not insurmountable. The thought lightened my footsteps. Maybe that was how I came upon an unsuspecting figure skulking in the dark of a dry-stone wall at a bend of the road. I froze in the deep shadows cast by a clump of hawthorn. My approach appeared to be unnoticed.

I guessed that the stranger was a man, although the voluminous over-garment that he was wearing — either a mac or a loose light overcoat of some kind — made any determination of sex difficult. That, and the shock of dark curly hair I could see silhouetted against the stonework. What gave me real concern, however, was sight of the weapon he was steadying on a flat slab of limestone capping the wall where he crouched. He held a long barrelled pistol which, fortunately, was trained not in my direction but on something in the field beyond the wall.

I try to have recourse to firearms as seldom as possible, but over the last few years, at least, I have become more than passing familiar with the more popular hand-guns. But this was no Luger, Biretta, nor Smith & Wesson. It certainly bore no resemblance to the snub-nosed .38 which was my usual companion on field jaunts for INIT and which was now safely cached in my Hotel room. Now, this remarkably long-barrelled job brought no flash of recognition — until it was fired. Then, directly I heard the dull 'plop' I realised that the stranger was using an air-pistol. Within seconds of firing he had scrambled over the stone wall and I could just make out his shadowy figure, bent double, foraging around on the edge of a field of wheat.

"The farmer's not going to thank you for trampling his young crop down," I said conversationally, coming to stand in the same spot that he had just vacated.

"Who the hell are you, man?" came his reply as he straightened and faced me.

For now, standing with the moonlight full on him, I could see that he was a young coloured man, possibly in his early twenties. I also saw the long barrel of the air-pistol raise until it was aimed directly at my face.

"I wouldn't pull that trigger, old son," I said. "I'm not really worth the trouble. What were you after, a rabbit for the pot?"

"No, man, it was a bloody great hare. He jumped just as I fired. Reckon I missed 'im." He lowered the weapon and came slowly towards me.

"Is there enough power in that thing to stop a hare?"

"Yeah, if you get'm in the right spot. Rabbits an' pheasant is easy, but a hare can take a bit of stopping. Mind you, this," he hefted the air-pistol, "fires B.B.s."

"What are B.B.s?"

"Ball-bearings, o'course!"

"Sounds nasty. But do you live around here — or doing a spot of rustic moonlighting a step or two from home?" I asked.

"What's it to you, where I come from?" he said belligerently. "I weren't poaching. Farmer should be pleased that I take out some of the rabbits and such-like that nibble away at his young corn."

"It's none of my business," I agreed. "Just trying to be friendly."

I watched as he scrambled back over the wall. Under the large old overcoat he was wearing I could see that he was quite a well set-up young fellow. As he stood beside me I noticed that he had the lighter skin of mixed blood rather than the dark features of a full-blooded West Indian. But the way he eyed me as he backed off a pace didn't offer too much hope for the olive branch I had verbally thrust in his direction.

The first punch I blocked and the second hay-maker of a swing I ducked, and as he lumbered past, slightly off-balance from that last abortive punch, I whipped the blade of my right-hand to the side of his neck with sufficient force to tumble him to the ground.

"Christ, man, what was that, karate or somethin'?" he said, sitting up in the roadway and caressing the side and back of his neck as though uncertain of the present disposition of his cervical vertebrae.

"Something like that," I agreed cheerfully. "Here, care to have one of these? I haven't any cigarettes," and I offered him my case of small cigars, as he came to his feet again.

He regarded me suspiciously, as though wondering where the catch was.

"Go on, take one," I urged. "No hard feelings, surely — although your neck was thick enough to hurt my hand."

His teeth flashed like a row of miniature tombstones, as he grinned. "Cor, thanks. It's days since I had a smoke — and certainly nothing as ritzy, man, as one of these panatellas."

"Hard times?" I said, thumbing my lighter into flame and offering it to him.

"Out of work. Just another member of the great unemployed," he said bitterly. "But without the benefit of any dole money for a few weeks."

"You left the job, rather than the job leaving you?" I hazarded.

"Yeah, that's about right. The gaffer opened his dirty mouth once too often about coloured fellows — so I filled it for him."

"If no dole, how about National Assistance?"

"They can stuff that!" he said inelegantly. "I'd sooner starve than ask them for their bloody charity handouts."

"It's not charity. It's a right," I pointed out.

"Look 'ere, mister, besides being partly coloured I was born the wrong side of the blanket. That makes me a bastard, an' although I keep hearing about it not being of any cons'quence in these enlightened times there's still folk in these parts that look down their bloody noses at Ma and me," he paused. "At least, they did often give my mother the frozen an' frosty look, but now she's passed on. That only leaves this bastard to thumb his nose at 'em. They can keep their bloody charity money. I'll make out!"

"Some bastards are born — but far more are self-made," I murmured.

I could see he was working that one out as he paced along beside me as we trod the lane towards Upper Chilworth, then a low chuckle escaped him. "Yeah, I see what you mean — an' was my late gaffer one of the self-made variety, man!"

I suddenly stopped as a thought came to me. "Look here, old son. I don't even know your name, but I'm willing to trust you on a small job for me."

"The name's Andy — Andy Richards — at least that's the name on my birth 'stifficate. And providing the job's honest — well, reasonably straight anyway — you're on."

"Good, then this is it, Andy. I need someone to keep an eye on a girl for me."

"That don't sound like too hard a job," he grinned. "Could be quite pleasant, in fact. Who is it? Anyone I know?"

"Miss Judy Quinton . . ."

A low whistle escaped him. "You mean one of the old Judge's daughters? Man, I sure do admire your taste. Although from all I've heard about the old man he's definitely one of those self-made types you just mentioned."

"You could well be right," I agreed.

"But do you know where he lives — a step or two back down this road?"

"I know the place. An' I know those two daughters of his. Say, they're both really good lookers — an' so much alike. Although I've always thought the younger one was likely to be a bit more fun than the older one, who strikes me as being a whole lot quieter."

So the news of Janet's death hadn't broken yet, I thought. But I decided it was best to level with young Andy.

"I'm afraid the younger girl, Janet Quinton, is dead. She was found murdered this morning."

"Christ, and you want me to play watchdog for the older girl? No thanks, mister, I don't want to get mixed up in that sort of aggro with the cops."

"There'll be no trouble for you on that score, Andy. Look, how much longer before you can claim dole money?"

"Three — four weeks."

"Right, then I'll pay you the equivalent of whatever dole money you would expect to receive, plus an extra bonus for weekend work. What do you say?"

"I'm not certain ... You sure this is straight?"

"Nothing outside of the law, by even the tiniest fraction," I assured him. "I would just feel happier if there was someone I could trust keeping an eye out for Judy Quinton. You'd not be able to do much during the daytime when she drives out, of course, but if you could watch out for things during the hours of darkness — say from 11 p.m. until 5 a.m. — I'd be grateful."

"Say, you a cop, yourself?" And as I shook my head. "Then you're stuck on the girl, ain't you?"

"You could say we're good friends."

"Good friends, my eye," he grinned. "Cor, what we blokes don't do for a skirt ... All right, guv, you're on. I'll begin tonight — in fact, right now."

"You will? Thanks. If you can patrol the grounds quietly, keeping an eye on the house. Anything suspicious, get on to me straight away. Don't attempt to tangle with anyone yourself. I'm staying at the Bellevue Hotel. Here's the 'phone number," I took a card from my wallet and handed it to him. "And here's a tenner for initial working expenses."

"Hey, that's good of you, man! There's a 'phone-box a hundred yards or so down the lane from the Quinton place. You want I should call you no matter what time o' night it is?"

"Yes, Andy. You see something you don't like — you call me."

He suddenly grinned again with a flash of teeth that should have netted him a fortune in any dentifrice advert. "An' s'posing the old Judge reckons he sees something suspicious and sneaks up behind me and puts the barrels of a shotgun up my jacksie?"

"If you're daft enough to let him get that close to you — then call me, old son — just call me."

"Right, then I'm starting me new job now," he said, then paused and stuck out a hand. "Care to shake on it, guv? You don't sound like a bleedin' toff — at least not most of the time — but for my money you *are* a toff."

"Flattery will get you anywhere," I murmured. "And by the way, for non-urgent messages, a scribbled note dropped in at the Hotel desk will reach me. Or, if you wander over in that direction at any time, call in and we'll have a drink together."

"What, at the Bellevue?"

"Sure, why not?"

"Say, things are looking up," he grinned again, and with a nod of his curly head, turned about and started back the way we had just come.

I watched him for a moment as he trudged off up the lane, and only then noticed the tail-feathers of a pheasant sticking out from one of the capacious pockets of his coat. He may have missed the hare, but it looked as though he had something for the pot. I wondered whether I had been wise in trusting an untried youngster with the task of looking out for Judy, but consoled myself with the thought that young Andy was better than having no one on watch. For of one thing I was quite sure; there was a particularly vicious form of villainy abroad in these rustic parts.

5

THE Cotswold bird-life disturbed me soon after the crack of dawn. I didn't exactly hear dawn arrive, you understand, although I could just make out the pearly-grey sky on the high horizon, but I sure enough heard our feathered friends in full song. However, I was having none of it. Skipping across to the window I tugged at curtains that I had been too lazy to close before, and then slid swiftly back between the sheets. Truth to tell, the last five or six weeks had been a hectic time and my sleep quota had suffered severely. Since this trip was, in part, a holiday, I rolled over, buried the O'Hara cheek in its previous indentation in the pillow and didn't surface again until 9 ack-emma.

Having bathed and performed the usual morning toiletries, plus applying a new dressing to the knife wound that had scored my ribs, I ordered a full breakfast to be sent up to my room and leisurely dressed myself.

Half-an-hour later, with the main protein course finished, I was just topping up with carbohydrates when, about to demolish a second slice of toast and marmalade, the telephone rang. My first thought was that Andy had something urgent to report, late in the morning though it was for him. But no, it was Courtney Fisk's voice that burbled over the line.

"Your uncle has just arrived. Shall I send him up?"

"My uncle?"

"Yes, he said that although you weren't expecting him you would know who he was. Not much family resemblance I must say. He's such a short gentleman — and equally short in manner."

"Ask him if he's Uncle Norman, will you, please?"

Within a few seconds, Courtney was

reporting back. "It is indeed, sir . . . I had him seated down here in the lounge, but I'm afraid he's already on his way up to you."

"That sounds like a man I know," I murmured. And upon opening the door, at a peremptory knock a couple of minutes later, my worst fears were realised. There in the flesh — what little there was of it — stood Sir Norman Norrick, and if you don't mind, we'll forget the string of letters that further embellish his name.

"Well, O'Hara, don't block the bloody doorway! Let me in!" he snapped.

Standing dutifully to one side I allowed the diminutive figure of my boss to gain access to Room No. 6.

"Breakfast in your room, eh? And at nearly ten o'clock in the morning! Will all this go down on your expense sheet?"

"Out working until the small hours, Sir Norman," I said virtuously. "But why the sudden honour of a visit?"

And indeed it was unusual, for never before had I known the head of the British section of INIT to make a field call. The 'Gnome' as he was known by the rest of the boyos, and the few colleens who slaved away risking life and limb — and the odd touch of purgatory at his direction — was definitely a desk-man. Standing some five-feet-two-inches in his built-up shoes, with a leathery face that owed much to a lengthy sojourn in the tropics as well as a regular acquaintance with near neat gin, his fringe of grey hair and heavily freckled tonsure gave him a benign look. Only the shrill snap of his voice gave any inkling of his true character. The 'Gnome' used his head for more than keeping his ears apart. It housed one of the most scheming, conniving brains that it had ever been my misfortune to come up against. And when you remember that I was supposed to be on his side, you could only fear for his enemies.

Feeling rather like the butler in

a British farce, I said, "Was there something — er — special, Sir?" And whenever I demeaned myself thus, I always mentally spelt the 'Sir' as *c-u-r*.

"It's about the murder of this Quinton girl — y'know, Judge Quinton's daughter. He knows too many people in high places and already he's stirring up the frigging sediment. We've got to come up with the answers to this one soon, O'Hara. Those rapacious sods at the Ministry are always looking for excuses to tighten our purse strings. It won't look good for us if we muff this one."

"Are you sure that this murder is marked down for INIT to investigate?" I asked. "It could be just a regular police job."

"No way!" he snarled. "This murder — and the latest killing of a chap called Warren, out Bibury way — are somehow tied in with this hellishly new narcotic caper that's surfacing here. Take my word for it," one forefinger tapped significantly at his domed forehead, "I sense it here!"

With this, he seized my last slice of toast, spread it liberally with butter, piled up the marmalade and then started his dentures chomping, whilst he seated himself on a corner of the table, legs a-swinging. Sitting there, all he needed was a pointed scarlet cap and frogged coat to look more like a garden gnome than some of the pseudo, plastic variety.

For the seconds that it took him to dispose of the remains of my breakfast, there was silence between us, broken only by the 'crunch' of rapidly disappearing toasted bread. Removing a snowy-white handkerchief that looked like the winning competitor in a T.V. washing-powder advertisement, from the sleeve of his impeccably-cut dark grey suit, he dabbed fastidiously at his cherubic little mouth.

"Anything new about the drug scene here?" I ventured.

"The buggers have come up with

something really diabolical. It appears to be a heroin-based concoction with — so far unknown to us — some form of additive that markedly increases the dependancy for any misguided clot that tries the stuff. Three or four normal doses, if they inject, and they're hooked. Takes a little longer if they sniff or smoke the muck."

"But they've been cutting 'H' with other stuff for years," I said. "Only a few months ago when top-quality heroin was hard to get, the traffickers were cutting it with caffeine . . . Now that the 'Poppy Barons' out East have released more of their stock — having upped the price for themselves — there's less pressure on them to keep the supply up at street-level."

"You're quite right about more of the high grade heroin — the white not the brown — finding its way to the western world. Last week we stopped a large Continental lorry that had just made the crossing to Sheppey in Kent. Stowed away around the vehicle, in the spare wheel and other unlikely places, over one hundred Kilos of pure heroin was discovered. Think of it, on the streets that amount would be worth some ten million quid ... And d'you know where the lorry was destined? To Cheltenham, right here in Gloucestershire."

"You wouldn't think they'd bother to cut the stuff when there's so much profit in the trade."

"Oh, there's bloody high overheads for them to contend with. They have palms to grease all the way along the line, remember," said the Gnome, and then paused and gave me a look in which I could almost read compassion. "Y'know, it's likely that this new stuff — the boffins have nicknamed it 'Mega-H' — has been around for longer than we've been aware of. We now know that in the beginning they may have been experimenting with whatever they were adding to the heroin to ginger it up. Analysts are still working on it and we now believe that a sudden rise in the death of addicts on the Channel Islands was helped along by a much stronger mixture than is now being offered. I'm afraid that your sister, Maureen, may well have been one of those unfortunates who were literally poisoned."

Although I've been trained to kill in many unpleasant but efficient ways, I pride myself on being able to keep any urge for mayhem well in check. But I must confess that memory of my young sister's last few days in that Guernsey hospital, still brought out an atavistic streak in me that would have had me reaching out for a stone-axe — or even half a house-brick — with which to batter in the skulls of all the unknown swines responsible for bringing her to such agony and final degradation.

"How far-reaching is trafficking in this new stuff — this 'Mega-H'?" I asked.

"Throughout most of the Western countries — and growing steadily. Certainly, Duclos of the French team and Wainwright in the States have reported an increasing use, while Heney of West Germany 'phoned me only yesterday to say that they had found several kilos of the drug concealed in a consignment of wigs that were being imported into his country. The worst aspect of the whole frigging business is that it seems to be ensnaring the young — especially the student intelligentsia of our populations. And its either killing them off at an escalating rate or leaving them as mindless zombies without wills to call their own."

"Surely the British end of this is based in London, Liverpool, Glasgow, or even Brum? Why have you directed me to this backwater? It's pleasant enough here, I'll warrant you that, but I would like to see more of the action so far as this particular caper is concerned. There must be a few Big Boys, untouched to date, whose necks I'd cheerfully like to have a hand in screwing."

"I've no doubt about that. You can

be a spiteful bastard, at times," agreed Sir Norman, cheerfully. "But take my word for it that you're in the right place, at the moment. You were sent here originally because of something that young Archie Clay in the Scrubs squeaked. In the last few days he's been — er — encouraged to tell us more. He's sure that there's something big in the narcotics world building up right here in Gloucestershire. He said something about the Cotswold Connection."

"Hey, dammit! Don't they know that some of the Royals live in this part of the country?"

"That's hardly likely to dissuade some of the villains who're banking on quick and hefty profits."

"But can we trust Archie Clay?" I asked.

"Normally, I wouldn't trust that evil little sod with the smallest coin of the realm," the Gnome admitted. "But if his finger has pointed us in the right direction and we can smash this

Mega-H ring he's down to receive a generous slice of remission. At the moment, as his sentence stands, if he does all the 'bird' that he's due for, he'll be well on into middle-age before he slops-out for the last time."

"Has he been able to throw any light on these two recent murders?"

"Not a dicky-bird about them, so far."

"I suppose they could be just coincidence — a lover's tiff that got out of hand?" I suggested.

"Could be, but I've a feeling in my old bones that there's some connection," he said, thoughtfully. "But whether it's something got screwed up with the main set-up, or something amiss with some subsidiary ring I've no way of knowing, at the moment . . . Do *you* think it's a case of unbridled passion that got way out of hand?"

"Not really. But if the killings are tied in with the drug connection here, it's been a clumsy error on their part. Certainly, the girl was a junkie — and they've stirred up the local police — "

"And the man, Gary Warren, was also an addict," he said, "but at the most, if either Janet Quinton or Warren were involved in drugs it was probably only as small-time pushers. More probably they were just hooked on the bloody stuff, themselves."

"By the way, I saw James Luckin at the village pub, last night," I said, changing conversational direction slightly. "I gather that he's been quite active in these parts lately. The dead girl saw him fairly regularly. He also tried to put the black on Judy Quinton over some porno photos of her sister, that he reckons to have."

"Lucky Jimmy — that ponced up pimp!" exploded my diminutive boss with a customary spate of colourful invective. "That man's about as much use to the human race as a syphilitic camel. Why we haven't been able to nail him before now, I'll never know," and he glowered at me as though I was the chief cause of our Jimmy's collar remaining unfelt.

"Well, he's a scoundrel sure enough, but a blasted clever one. He always manages to stay on the periphery of any skulduggery that's around — "

"Periphery, my backside!" retorted the Gnome, inelegantly. "He's the bloody big fat spider that's at the centre of too many dirty webs. Drugs, hard-porno, prostitution, the protection racket — you name it, and he's somewhere in the background, scraping in the loot."

"Would he be head-man of this latest narcotic scare?" I asked, already with my own views on that subject.

"Not a chance. This Mega-H caper is too big for Jimmy Luckin," replied the Gnome, thoughtfully running a forefinger from the bridge to the tip of his little beak of a nose. "But, although he may not be Mister Big I'll wager he's got his dirty fat paws dug well in there . . . By the way, was that woman of his around — the one who breaks in the young tarts for him?"

I grimaced. "You mean Bordello Lil? No, I've seen no sign of that painted popsie, but he seems to have a new heavy serving as his chauffeur."

"A big Australian bugger?"

"Could be. Can't say for sure because I've never heard him talk. Only saw him once, giving his boss the nod just before Judy Quinton turned up at the *Pig and Parsnip*."

"If it is the Australian — and I've a notion it must be — watch out if you ever have to tangle with him, O'Hara. He's really rough."

"Thanks for the warning," I said drily. "Who is he — just a new recruit to Lucky Jimmy's band of protection thugs?"

The Gnome nodded. "Name of Moxey — Eddie Moxey. He arrived here a couple of months back via the States. Nothing excitingly villainous known about him so far. Could, of course, be travelling under an alias. But he's a hard nut."

"What makes you think he's so

tough, Sir Norman?"

"He's been acting part-time bouncer at Jimmy's gambling club. I'm told that there should have been a case of assault and G.B.H. brought against him. That little affray was finally hushed up because Jock Steen's manager decided that it wouldn't make all that good publicity for his boy . . ."

"Jock Steen — the current contender for the British Heavyweight title?"

There was a gleam of spiteful amusement in the Gnome's china-blue eyes. "That's the boyo. Steen lost a packet at Jimmy's club, and carrying a little too much alcohol under his belt, decided to remonstrate with the management regarding the dealing at one of the tables. Well, Eddie Moxey worked him over in a most salutary fashion. Not, you understand, strictly according to the Marquis of Queensbury. But as I heard it, he was quite devastating in his own way. One reason why Steen's training has been put back for a couple of months."

"Jock's no angel in the ring, himself," I murmured. "I saw his last fight. The referee must have suffered from myopia."

"Oh, I've no doubt that Steen deserved all he had coming to him, but watch out for Moxey. The fellow's as strong as an ox and soaks up punishment like a sponge. So be warned, O'Hara. The team can't afford expensive hospital bills for its personnel."

"If he so much as looks my way, I'll beetle off in the other direction," I assured my boss, gravely.

"Like you did in Guernsey, when that thug tried to expose your liver to some air and sunshine," the Gnome grunted. "Don't under-rate the opposition, Michael."

I blinked at his use of my Christian name. I was surprised that the Gnome even knew it. Such a change from O'Hara do this, O'Hara do that. Sometimes, even, O'Hara *don't* do that!

"Take my word for it, this latest

drug caper is the most serious threat that the Western World has faced," he continued. "Have you seen the latest addiction figures for Britain, alone, this year?"

"At least 25 percent up on last year's total," I volunteered. "And that's only for known addicts."

"S'right," he nodded. "While Wainwright tells me that the figures in the States, this year, have escalated far beyond ours. Of course, cocaine is high on their list, being smuggled in so easily from the coca-growing areas of South America. That's the worst of having drug-growing smallholdings on your back doorstep. But now, along with hashish and all the other junk that's being pushed with such growing frequency in the US of A are signs of a rapidly increasing use of Mega-H. Wainwright swears that it's being smuggled in from France or Belgium. Duclos says that he's sure it was being circulated from Belgium, but trafficking in the drug has almost ceased there for the moment. Unfortunately, as I've said, this dope has such a rapidly addictive hold and such mind-blowing properties that, among the student population in particular, there has been a frightening rise in rapes, suicides, murders and other acts of violent mayhem, as much because of hellish withdrawal symptoms as anything else. And now we're finding the drug surfacing in our big cities."

"Well, I suppose the bulk of our hashish comes from the Middle East and most of our heroin from the Far East. Is some Eastern syndicate trying the market in various countries?" I asked.

"At this moment we just don't know for sure. But it's my guess that although the heroin is coming from Hong-Kong, Pakistan, Vietnam, or where-ever, the actual manufacture of Mega-H — the incorporation of other drug or drugs with the heroin — is taking place much closer to home," Sir Norman said.

"As close as here in the Cotswolds?"

The Gnome shrugged his narrow shoulders. "Who really knows? All we have to go on is that squeal from Archie Clay. It didn't make sense to us when he fingered the Cotswolds as being the centre for a new British-based drug-ring. But our Archie was quite adamant, and since the little rat was well up in the drug caper in London, before Mr. Justice Quinton sent him down for that long stretch tied in to an inter-gang killing, we figured that he knew what he was talking about."

"It was Judge Quinton who sent Archie down?" I asked.

"Sure, but don't read anything other than coincidence into that. Remember, old Quinton has come down heavily on scores of villains in his time — and on none more so that those connected with illegal narcotic dealings."

"True enough," I agreed. "Didn't Archie whisper any names, at all? Even one would help at this stage."

"Not a single name. All he could — or would — tell us is that a newcomer was about to set up in a big way in this country. Name unknown — at least so Archie maintains — but the centre of the bloody ring was likely to be here in Gloucestershire."

"Well, I'll just have to carry on digging around," I said. 'And hope it's not my own grave I'm digging', I thought.

"You do just that, m'boy. Have a right good nose around. We've every confidence in you," he replied.

"Can I ask for any help in the field?"

He grinned puckishly. "Ask away, O'Hara. No harm in asking. Can't spare anyone for you, though."

So that was it. I was expected to sew this one up all on my jack. I felt sure that this was the Gnome penny-pinching again. We may have only half-a-dozen peripatetic operatives in Britain — backed up by at least twice that number of desk-borne personnel — but surely there was at least one other member of the team who could be charged with the job of minding my back.

"How about Roderick or Beale?" I suggested.

"Both in Glasgow, dear boy. There are other situations that we have to investigate, y'know. We're checking on some very high-grade cocaine that's found its way to those parts."

"Then how about Owen?" I persisted. "Or has he chucked the job in after the way you set him up as the sacrificial goat in the Guernsey fracas?"

"Hmm! Sorry to say that Owen is still in hospital. What we thought was a simple case of concussion regrettably turned out to be a fracture of the skull. The poor man must have less of a thick head than I thought."

"The brutal way they sapped him and left him for dead, I'm not surprised," I said frostily. "Why the hell we don't all duck and run for cover when the going gets rough, I'll never know. When our efforts go off course we don't receive much sympathy."

"On the contrary," replied my diminutive boss, plucking at his little rosebud lip. "Although every one of our operatives have been chosen because of their physical ability to — er — face adversity — we feel things very, very strongly when they fall foul of the opposition. But come, m'boy, this will probably prove to be a simple enough case. I've no doubt you'll have it all nicely wrapped up within a week or two. I have complete faith in your competence, O'Hara. I've not forgotten how you came to Owen's help when the ordure started hitting the fan at the close of the little Channel Island affair."

I bit back a few succinct four-letter words which I could have used to describe the staff-work back of my last field-outing on the Gnome's behalf. I realized that I would have to accept the inevitable. No matter what mire I landed in while trying to unravel this Cotswold drug connection, so far as my little pip-squeak boss was concerned I was out on my own.

"OK, if it's down to me, I'll have to go it alone," I said sourly.

"That's the spirit," replied Sir Norman, slipping down from the corner of the table and coming to his child-size feet. "Of course, if you think the manure is about to be thrown around in too liberal a manner, you can always give me a call."

"Where will you be?" I asked suspiciously, remembering how unusual was his visit here to Upper Chilworth.

"For the next few days I'll be at my weekend place in Cheltenham. A few days' respite from the burdens of office, you understand. Don't disturb me unless it's a matter of earth-shattering importance." With which, and a bird-like nod of his head, he left me.

Several minutes passed before I realized that not only was it news to me that the Gnome had a pad out here in Cheltenham, as well as a luxury apartment in Kensington, but he had failed to offer me his address for the next few days. I skipped to the window in time to see his spanking new Rover disappear down the drive. Five minutes later and I was on the 'phone to the London office.

"No, Mister O'Hara, I've absolutely no idea where Sir Norman is staying," said his plump little secretary, who I rather thought was her boss's current delight. "The poor man's been working so hard. It's only fair that he should be able to forget the pressures of this business for a week or two. 'Bye now!"

A week or two! The conniving little clown was obviously set for a very long weekend!

6

"ISN'T it amazing what tricks genes can play," observed Courtney Fisk, as he served me a midday aperitif at the Hotel bar. "Your Uncle bears very little resemblance to you. He's such a small man."

And that, I thought, was rather good, coming from the Hotel Manager who was scarcely knee-high to a grasshopper, himself."

"My mother's side of the family," I said, recovering my nose from a reasonably dry Martini. "They would take up smoking at an early age. You know how it stunts the growth." Leaving him to ponder on this, I took my drink out to the verandah which skirted the south side of the Bellevue.

Seated there in the June sunshine, I let the grey matter gently tick over, correlating the few facts that, so far, I had to work on. A discreet cough at my elbow made me aware that apple-cheeked Millie Gray, the waitress, was offering me a copy of the morning newspaper.

"It's all there, sir," she said. "Thought you might like to read about it. Fancy Chilworth getting into the news like that. There's a nice likeness of Mr. Justice Quinton on page two."

Thanking her, I skimmed the front page of the tabloid. Sensationally written, it told me nothing new. Page two, however, did indeed have a clear picture of the Judge. It showed the dour, smooth-shaven face of a man well into his sixties, with the uncompromising jaw-line and chin that reminded me of the toe of a size eleven army boot. I could well imagine that many a villain had inwardly quaked to see that visage peering at him from beneath the wig of justice.

Both murders had been reported in the paper, but had been displayed as separate news items, under the by-line of 'Special Correspondent'. Strangely enough, I had seen no sign of Press activity in the hotel, and had no doubt that Inspector Marlow had been keeping a low profile about the killings. With the newspaper folded again, I was about to let the grey matter resume its ponderings when a low whistle from the lane, which curved round the perimeter of the Hotel ground, attracted my attention. At first I failed to recognise the neatly-dressed figure, but directly I realised that it was Andy, my amateur watch-dog, I beckoned him to join me on the veranda.

"You couldn't have had much sleep last night, or rather, this morning," I smiled. "How about a drink?"

Minutes later, with my own fair hands, I brought him the pint of bitter that he requested.

"What gives, Andy? Anything to report?"

"Yes, but I'm not sure how important it is. I think someone was casing Judge Quinton's place in the small hours. He was a big geezer, with a back the width of a barn door. I didn't fancy tangling with 'im but I watched real careful."

"Would you recognise him again?"

"'Fraid not. He was in some sort o' dark uniform with a peaked cap pulled down low so that his face were in shadow."

"It sounds like a character called Eddie Moxon. Maybe it's as well that you didn't tackle him. D'you think he saw you?"

"No way. I followed him all round the outside of the house though. He tried some of the doors and windows — not as if he were trying to break in y'understand, more like he was looking for something."

"Burglar alarms, I wouldn't be surprised," I said. "He was casing the place, all right."

"Apart from that he didn't do anything out of the way, guv. It must've taken him near twenty minutes to check up on things an' then — he just went."

"Thanks, Andy. I'll go on look-out tonight," I said, thoughtfully. "You'll be able to have a good night's kip."

"You're just trying to do me out of my job," he grinned. "You can be my assistant, if you like, but no way am I going to lose the first bit of honest employment I've had in months."

"Hey! You told me you had only been unemployed for a week or so."

"Oh, that job! I was talking about *honest* work. Not leaning over backwards to gyp the customers, like my last gaffer expected me to."

"And what line of work was that?"

"Sorry, guv, no names. Let's just say that I had to come on so strong with some of the punters that I was becomin' ashamed of myself."

"Fair enough. But I think I had better straighten you on a few facts, then you'll know just what you're letting yourself in for." I paused for a moment, wondering how far I dare explain things to him. I liked young Andy a hell of a lot and didn't want to see him beaten up, or chivved, or worse, while he was helping me in all innocence. On the other hand I had no wish to completely blow my cover.

"I don't know how much you know about drug-trafficking," I said, at last. "But I've heard that there's some sort of gang operating locally. This could be the reason for Janet Quinton being murdered — maybe she was on to something. However, since I'm a close friend of Judy Quinton (and that was taking a lot for granted) I thought it best to keep an eye out for her."

"I can't believe that — about a drug gang in these parts. I would surely have heard. Some of the kids may pop the odd pill — and in Gloucester there's a tear-away bunch that are heavy into 'grass' — but I shouldn't think there's anything more serious than that. When I was a teenager I had the odd puff of hash myself, man, but I knew that it would upset Ma if she got to hear of it so I cut it out."

"Wise lad," I murmured. "In more

cases than I like to recall I've known the use of so-called soft drugs leading on to the hard stuff, and addiction."

My companion was silent for a moment. "I know I'm not all that bright," he said at last. "But how is it that folks can't say 'no' to something that's no good for 'em?"

By way of an answer, I took a packet of panatellas from my pocket and offered him one. When a trail of blue smoke was curling above his head as he puffed luxuriously at the slim cigar, I ostentatiously closed the packet and returned it to my pocket.

"Not having one yourself, guv?"

"I've just said 'no' to myself, Andy. How long have you been a regular smoker?"

"Started while I was a kid at school. Used to slip out o' the playground, follow a hedge round into the woods an' have a sly puff." His teeth suddenly flashed. "I often forgot to return to school for the rest o' that day."

"Would you find it difficult to give

up smoking?" I persisted.

"I've had to go without when funds were low, from time to time. It was never too pleasant."

"Smoking is a comparatively mild form of addiction, compared to the utter dependency that hard drugs produce."

"Come off it, man. I'm never a 'junkie' because I like a fag!"

"The unfortunate fact, young Andy, is that most of us have addictions — mild though they may be — that we fail to recognise."

My companion grinned again. "Guess you can say I'm addicted to eating and breathin'."

I smiled. "Don't forget that there are some slimmers who've taken things too far and they are now addicted to *not* eating. But I was thinking more about tobacco and alcohol, and even, to a much lesser extent, tea and coffee — and even sugar. How many people do you know, who say that they have a 'sweet tooth' and can't resist cakes and confectionery? To some degree we all seem to have our own addictions — although no way are these likely to bring the degradation that reliance on hard drugs will produce."

Andy removed the half-smoked panatella from his lips and eyed it speculatively.

"Finish it," I smiled. "I'm not getting at you, old son, but just trying to explain about this rotten drug business."

"When you talk about hard drugs you mean cocaine, I suppose?" he said.

"That and heroin are the two most troublesome ones at the moment. In the past there has been concern about cannabis, LSD, or the heroin substitutes like methadone and amphetamines. But these days it's 'C' and 'H' that are causing most trouble in the Western world."

"Mm, sometimes at a disco, in Cheltenham or Gloucester, I've had little packets of stuff offered me," my companion said. "I was never interested enough to try 'em — in any case, the prices were always rather steep. But tell me, Mike, where do these hard drugs come from? Do they have to make 'em in the lab'ratory?"

"The final, refining process has to be done by people who have the know-how, but the raw materials for both cocaine and heroin are derived from plants. Strangely enough, from plants that normally grow on opposite sides of the world."

Andy took a healthy swig of bitter. "Tell me about them, guv, if you can spare the time. I may not be well-educated, but I'm always willing to learn."

"Well, in the first place, you've to remember that although these drugs are abused they are extremely valuable to the medical world, when correctly prescribed. Cocaine begins its life as leaves of the coca plant, much of it being grown by peasant farmers in Peru and Bolivia. It's harvested some three or four times a year, requiring about 150 kilos of leaves to produce 1 kilo of cocaine. Of course, the Indians of South America have known of the coca plant's properties for centuries. They chew the leaves to fight off fatigue, especially at high altitudes."

"Our junkies don't chew leaves."

"No," I smiled. "First, the leaves are dried to make them pliable. Then they are soaked in a solution, usually of potash, paraffin and water. Once the alkaloids have been freed, the fluid and leaves are removed, leaving a residual brown paste. And at this stage the price starts escalating. Leaves, as harvested, are sold for just over one-pound sterling a kilo; the brown paste changes hands at about £200 a kilo."

"And is that it?" asked Andy. "Is that the actual stuff they inject or sniff?"

"No, the manufacturing process has a further stage. Bent chemists treat the brown paste so that it yields a crystalline alkaloid that is often over 90 percent pure cocaine and now fetches over

£3,000 a kilo when sold to dealers. By the time the drug reaches the streets it has been 'cut' so that it probably is then only 10 percent pure."

"You mean they mix somethin' with the cocaine so that they can rake in even more profit?"

"That's right, Andy. I recently saw figures from America that showed how a single kilo of pure cocaine, when treated, could produce over half a million pounds at street level. Weight for weight, the drug is worth more than three times the value of gold."

"Jeeze! No wonder it's become such a big business, man. But if they weaken its strength by cutting it can it be all that dangerous to use?"

"It's said not to create such dependency as heroin, but it can still be a killer. It badly damages the nose after being continually 'snorted' and produces horrific hallucinations. While those who inject the drug in order to produce a quicker 'high' further imperil themselves from the contamination of dirty syringes — as well as from some of the muck that unscrupulous dealers use to 'cut' the drug in order to increase street-side profits. Finally, after prolonged use, breathing failure can be caused by paralysis of the respiratory centres."

"Say, man who'd reckon that leaves of a plant could be so deadly?"

"If anything, heroin is even more frightful in its results."

"Then tell me about that one, as well, guv," said Andy, cupping his chin in his hand.

"I'm not boring you?"

"No ruddy fear! If you must know I've never had anyone take the trouble to tell me about things the way you do. Ma used to try, but although she were as bright as a button about everyday things, she wasn't really int'rested in matters that took her too far away from her kitchen."

"Well, she doesn't seem to have made too bad a job of bringing you up."

"She did her best. Reckon she had to be both mother an' father to me. I miss her, y'know."

"No girl friends?"

"No," he grinned. "No money!"

"Now you're being cynical, young Andy."

"Mebbe so. But you were going to tell me about this other drug — heroin."

"Here goes then. Heroin is derived from another plant — the poppy. Fields of them are grown in countries of the Near and Far East for the opium content of their seed-pods."

"Opium — ain't that the stuff the Chinese smoke?"

"Not just the Chinese, I'm afraid, and our own history so far as the Opium Trade was concerned is not all that lily-white. But that was many years ago when a different morality prevailed. Not that human nature seems to have changed all that much."

"Then this heroin is made from the poppy-seeds something like cocaine is made from coca-leaves?"

"A similar refinement takes place — and there's certainly the same rapid increase in price. They don't use the actual seeds, Andy, but cut into the seed pod so that the resulting rather sticky sap can be collected. This congeals and forms opium, which in its turn is refined by chemists into heroin. Powdered heroin is used for injections while small lumps of the stuff can be smoked. Just like cocaine, it becomes terribly addictive for the regular user, and soon begins to play hell with even the strongest constitutions."

"And you reckon there's a local gang pushing both these drugs, guv?"

"No, not both of them. But we've reason to believe that some clever swine — probably a bent chemist-type — has found a way of producing a form of heroin that's even more mind-blowing and addictive than the normal street stuff. Lord knows how much street pushers are charging for this new, pepped-up dope."

"It's really serious?"

"It is that, Andy. Not just here in the immediate area of the Cotswolds — although that would be bad enough. But if this new drug, they call Mega-H, can cause the rapid addiction that I've been told about, then foolish folk in all our big cities — especially those youngsters who are maybe bored with things and want to experiment — will be in grave risk. As a matter of fact, I rather expect this part of the country is being used only as a centre from which the drug can be distributed."

"And because it's such a profitable caper, anyone trying to poke his nose into things is likely to get it severely bent, eh, man?"

"That's the size of it, old son," I agreed. "The big boys of illicit drug trafficking can boast of millionaire status if business proceeds according to plan. Their rich pickings come not so much from the 'high' that use of drugs can produce but from the dependence that causes the addict to sell his soul for the next fix."

"You sure as hell make it sound serious," Andy said, taking another long pull at his bitter that lowered it to within an inch from the bottom of the glass. "You certain sure you ain't a cop?"

"No, I'm not with the police. If you must know, my own young sister died because of her drug addiction. In the beginning, and unknown to her, I'm sure, she was unsuspectingly 'fed' a few doses of the drug — possibly this new Mega-H — and that was the beginning of the end for her."

"Aw, hell, I'm sorry, Mike! I can see why you want to catch up with the guy concerned."

"He's already been caught up with!" I said, soberly. "He was one of the gang who was pushing the stuff in the Channel Islands — in Guernsey, to be precise. My sister used to work as a secretary on the island. But the only pushing that that character's engaged in these days is pushing up the daisies."

Andy gave a low whistle. "Did you snuff him?"

"I had to." Even as I spoke I could feel the plaster strapping pulling at the side of my rib-cage. "It was as much a question of self-defence as revenge," I lied — for no way had I been willing to let that particular scum do his spell of porridge and then be released to continue screwing up more young lives. No amount of corrective detention ever seems to deter those involved in illegal drug-trafficking from renouncing such a lucrative caper.

"However," I continued. "I must point out that you could be involved in some danger if you want to go along with me for the next few weeks."

My companion drained the dregs of his bitter, ran the tip of his tongue over his lips to savour the last of the flavour, and then said, "I really want this job, Mike. Don't worry about me. I'm going into this with my eyes open now. And, man, from all you've told me it seems the most worthwhile employment I've had so far. So, thanks — count me in!"

"I'm the one who's grateful, Andy. I've a strong notion that before long I'm going to need someone I can trust."

"I'll help all I can," he replied, coming to his feet and thrusting out a hand. "I'll be off now — a bit of shopping I should see to. Where do we meet tonight, and at what time?"

"The same place where I first saw you, taking a pot-shot at that hare," I said, pleased to feel the strength of his hand-shake. "I'll try to make it around 11 o'clock tonight."

He nodded. "Be seein' you. 'Bye for now, guv."

I watched as he took a short cut across the lawn, vaulted the dry-stone wall and set off down the lane. Later, with the inner-man suggesting that some form of midday sustenance would be in order, I was about to drift over to the hotel dining-room, when a police-car rounded a bend in the lane and turned in to the hotel forecourt. A uniformed copper was driving. He braked smartly, hopped out of the driving-seat and opened a rear door, first on the offside to allow Inspector Marlow to disembark and then round to the near-side to allow a tall, lean, slightly stoop-shouldered man to alight. I came to my feet. Noticing the movement, Marlow ushered the lean and hungry-looking gent in my direction.

As they drew nearer, I recognised the Inspector's companion, thanks to page two of that morning's newspaper. I was about to meet Mr. Justice Quinton in the flesh — and pretty sparing nature had been with that commodity so far as the Judge was concerned.

"This is the man — Michael O'Hara — who discovered Janet's body," Marlow opened the introduction.

Aggressive chin and beaked nose lent the Judge an odd Punch-like look. It was a characteristic that had not been overly marked in the full-face picture in the newspaper. His eyes, too, had a piercingly calculating look that I had not been able to appreciate before. It appeared to take him only a matter of a few seconds to sum me up — and he did not seem to be singularly impressed with what he saw.

Withdrawing his bony, claw-like fingers after a perfunctory handshake, he said, "So you're the fellow that Norrick sets so much store by."

There goes my cover again, I thought. But it was news that the Gnome had any regard for me.

"Hmph!" put in the Inspector. "Apparently, Mr. O'Hara is much thought of by the British section of INIT. Of course, it must have been pure coincidence that he should have booked in here at the Bellevue at the time of this unfortunate affair with your step-daughter, Judge."

Quinton's curiously light-grey eyes seemed to drill into me from under the iron-grey bushy brows. "As you say, Inspector, quite a coincidence." Then addressing me directly. "You're not here solely on vacation, O'Hara, are you?"

Uncertain just how much information he had been able to prise out of the Gnome I prevaricated somewhat. "In the beginning it was meant purely as a holiday. Sir Norman agreed that I could have time to recharge my batteries after my last little jaunt for him."

"That, of course, would be the Guernsey affair," snapped the Judge, thereby making it abundantly clear that he was well up with news of the Section's activities. "Was it necessary to break that man's neck?"

I felt my hackles rising. Not only did he know too dam' much but I didn't like the manner in which he aired his knowledge. "He fell awkwardly," I replied coldly. "And I wasn't greatly concerned about cushioning his fall at the time because he had just spent several wearisome minutes trying to stick his knife in my gizzard!"

"The man should have been brought to justice in the proper manner," said Quinton. "Not dismissed from this world in such a summary fashion . . . I suppose you were quite sure of his guilt?"

"He was as guilty as hell. If you haven't already seen it, my full report was lodged with Sir Norman."

"Perhaps this is not the best time or place," suggested Inspector Marlow placatingly.

"How about this fellow, Gary Warren?" said the Judge, changing the subject abruptly and choosing to ignore Marlow's soothing noises. "What d'you know about him, O'Hara?"

"Probably not so much as you know," I retorted icily. "He's just a name to me. Never set eyes on him, so far as I know."

"How about it, Marlow? Do we know anything about him? I saw him once or twice at my place until I made it clear that his absence was preferable to his presence there," the Judge said.

"He was sent down from Oxford about three years ago for a particularly unsavoury incident. Came from a good family well-connected with brokerage in Bristol. Too much of a black sheep, however, to be welcomed in the family fold. Served behind the bar here at the Hotel — not that he needed the money, judging by his clothes and his car, and his general high standard of living," the Inspector offered.

"Any connection with illegal drug business?" Quinton asked.

"Could well be, but we have no proof. Although judging by marks found on his body he was certainly injecting himself."

"What was he using?" I put in. "Cocaine or heroin?"

"Not sure at the moment," replied Marlow, heavily. "A double shot-gun blast didn't leave a pretty corpse. The doctor's still working on that question."

"Well, keep me posted," said his older companion. "Two murders in such a short space of time are very unsettling."

Was this the man who was supposed to be grieving over the death of a favourite step-daughter, I wondered? And then, almost as though he had read my thoughts, he said, "Young man, whoever took my daughter's life must be brought to book. You understand?

"Suppose he gets his neck broken accidentally?" I couldn't help murmuring.

It was as though he hadn't heard me. With a complete change of voice and manner — so different from the belligerency of his previous cross-questioning — he said. "I'd like both of you to come across to my place for lunch."

With an unspoken question I shot a glance in Inspector Marlow's direction. "I can't make it today, myself," he apologised hastily.

"Then you'll be able to drop O'Hara and myself off before returning to your duties, I trust?" And the voice was one that would brook no argument.

Which was why, a few moments later, I found myself seated in the passenger seat, alongside the uniformed driver, speeding through Upper Chilworth towards Judge Quinton's stately pile. And if you think that I was going to pass up this chance for a further meeting with Judy Quinton, you must be bonkers!

7

SHE was wearing a cream-coloured blouse and fawn slacks beneath a gaily-flowered smock; the smudge of paint on her cheek made me certain that Judy hadn't been expecting company.

"Why, hallo!" she said, meeting us in the hall and looking from her step-father to your humble in a rather nonplussed way.

"Lunch, Judy . . . What have you got for us, m'dear?" said the Judge.

"Lunch?" Her gorgeous eyes opened wide. "I — I've only some salad, home-made bread, ham and cheeses."

"Excellent, m'dear. And a bottle of that fruit wine that you produce so splendidly. Have you any of the mulberry left?" He turned to me. "We've a couple of mulberry trees in the garden, well over half-a-century old but always smothered with fruit in season."

This was a new side to the Judge. One I liked much better than his manner at our first meeting. As Judy left us to prepare our lunch he watched her affectionately.

"That girl's a treasure. Much more like her mother than poor Janet ever was," he confided. "She'll have a meal put together for us in double quick time."

"The, er, paint on her cheek — was she decorating?"

"Oh, that! No, I expect we interrupted her in her studio. Probably at work on something for her craft shop."

I couldn't keep the surprise from my voice. "Her craft shop?"

The Judge's bleak features softened to a smile. "No need for her to work, of course, but that's not Judy's way. She's built up a profitable little business in Cirencester. Mainly depends on the tourist trade — but offers decent enough things. Certainly far superior to the trash that some places try to peddle."

"Did your younger daughter have any interest in the craft business?" I asked.

"No. When my wife died she left both girls useful bequests. Judy set up her craft business while Janet went into partnership in a herbalist and health food business just outside Bibury. I've only been to see the place once. Never did meet her partner. They converted a couple of old barns — beyond Arlington Mill — into a warehouse and laboratory. Can't say I hold with all this modern craze for vitamin pills and health foods myself. Good, plain cooking has always served me well enough. The trouble is that I'm home so seldom that I can't enjoy it as often as I would like."

And it was some home that the Judge had! The dining-room where Judy finally set about laying table was an antique-lover's delight. There was nothing fake about the Sheraton,

Hepplewhite and Chippendale furniture here. The splendid dining-table and chairs must have seen a couple of centuries' use — just as the exposed beams in the ceiling above us would have seen generations come and go. The wide stone fire-place and chimney-breast housed a brilliant arrangement of early summer flowers at the moment, with a preponderance of fragrant roses of the old school, but the smoke-stained stones immediately surrounding the open hearth were mute evidence of many a roaring log-fire. The floral arrangement was housed in a large copper vessel and other pieces of antique copper gleamed warmly against the rough-hewn limestone. While shelves, from floor to ceiling, on each side of the chimney-breast, held expensive-looking collections of leather-bound books together with a miscellany of porcelain figures. At our feet a magnificent Turkish carpet gleamed deep crimson in the sunlight shafting in through the wide mullioned windows.

If the rest of the house was like this, then Mr. Justice Quinton's home was indeed his castle. My companion must have correctly interpreted my appreciative glances.

"You like the room?" he smiled.

"No Cotswold home should be without a dining-room like this," I assured him.

His lantern-jawed face softened strangely. "Five generations of my family have lived here. I'm prejudiced I know, but I love the old place. Mind you, the cost of its upkeep becomes an ever-increasing burden to bear . . . But if you've the time to spare I'll ask Judy to show you over the place, after lunch."

"And the garden, please." I murmured, with an eye now to the trim lawns and flourishing flower-beds seen framed through the windows.

"Of course," he said, and then excused himself as there came a call from his daughter — presumably in the kitchen now — asking for assistance in uncorking the wine.

During his brief absence I moved across the room to study a collection of miniatures arranged on the cream-washed wall between the two main windows. With the exception of three tiny landscapes and two portraits the miniatures mainly depicted flora, or wild birds and creatures in their natural habitats. I'm no great art buff, but I could recognise the skill and artistry which had produced such beautiful, small creations. I was particularly intrigued to see the range of materials on which the miniatures had been executed. Those painted on canvas were further enhanced by oval or oblong frames of gilt or polished wood. But the ones which really fascinated me were those which had been painted on tablets of wood or ivory, or polished slices of semi-precious stones.

"How d'you like them?" my host asked, as he rejoined me.

"They're really unique. Have you been collecting them for very long?"

"All of three years," he replied solemnly. "Ever since Judy finished at art college."

"All these are — her work?"

"Every one of them. She paints larger canvasses, but her miniatures are in such demand that they represent most of her work, these days."

"They deserve to be popular. They're charming."

"Tourists seem to think so," smiled Judy, re-entering the room. "It's nice to have a pleasant hobby that pays so handsomely. Do you really like them or were you just being your usual polite self?"

"I honestly think they are exquisite — and that's not a word I use more than once every leap-year."

"Which word — honestly or exquisite?" she asked impishly, retiring briefly again before returning with a well-stocked serving trolley, the contents of which she placed at strategic points around the dining-table.

* * *

"Neither Mrs. Dobson nor daughter here today?" asked the Judge, seating himself in what was obviously his customary chair at the head of the table and charging his plate with crisp salad, ham and cheese.

"I gave them both the day off," his step-daughter replied. "I wasn't expecting company. You're home much earlier than I thought possible."

"Sorry I was unable to get a message to you, m'girl."

And now for the first time since we had met I saw grief shadowing his eyes and realised that self-discipline had so far kept it in check. The old Judge was certainly not one to carry his heart on his sleeve!

For a long time there was an unbroken silence between us. I looked from father to step-daughter. Both heads were lowered over their plates as they toyed with their food in a desultory fashion.

"That was really most enjoyable," I said, at last, placing my eating-irons neatly on my now empty plate.

"More salad?" Judy asked, and as I gave a negative shake of my head she came to her feet. "There's a lemon sorbet here. Do have some," she paused to look across at the Judge, whose eyes were still lowered. "It's one of Daddy's favourite sweets."

At that moment the fluted notes of a door-chime sounded and excusing herself, she went to answer their summons. Now call it sixth-sense, déjà-vu or what you will, I just knew that those chimes meant trouble. The sound of a scuffle and a muffled exclamation at the door brought even my host sitting bolt upright in his chair. I was halfway out of mine when two boiler-suit clad figures, their noses grotesquely flattened by the balaclava type stockinette masks they wore, burst into the room.

The slimmer of the two held a lethal sawn-off shot-gun pointing towards

Judge Quinton and myself, the other man — a huge brute of a fellow — held Judy in front of him, one arm firmly about her writhing body and a hand clamped cruelly at her throat. Gently I subsided into my seat again. Arguments with sawn-off shot-guns at that range were just not on for this boyo.

"Wh-what is the meaning of this outrage?" spluttered the Judge.

"We've come to collect — you know what," came the slim one's muffled voice.

"Before you do any collecting how about telling that gorilla to take his hands off the girl. She won't scream now that we've been almost introduced," I said, reasonably.

At a nod from the slim gentleman the other removed his hand from Judy's throat but kept a firm grip about her body.

"Keep still, Judy, until we can sort this little lot out," I urged. Then, looking across at the old Judge I said, "Have you any idea what these two creeps are talking about?"

"He knows, all right," put in the talkative one. "Not only does he know what we want — but who wants it."

"You're talking in riddles," replied my host, distastefully.

"Then let me make our demands perfectly clear. Your late daughter stole something of ours that is extremely valuable to us. We happen to know that just before her regrettable demise she posted it, addressed to you at your London chambers."

"I still have no idea what you're talking about!" snapped the Judge. "Directly it was made possible for me I came straight on here from the Old Bailey."

I looked across at him. I was certain that the old boy was telling the truth. Whatever they were after, it was all Greek to him. The same message finally seemed to sink home with the shot-gun johnny. Following several moments of silence, he finally transferred the shot-gun to his left hand, a new trigger-finger taking up the strain with maddening ambidexterity, while his right-hand unzipped the top of his boiler-suit and retrieved a photograph from an inner pocket. With a skill that must have evolved from years of practice in some school playground he flicked the photograph so that it landed face upwards on the table between the Judge and myself. It was a glossy monochrome enlargement of a girl engaged in a sexually athletic manner with a particularly well-endowed young gentleman, whose greasy black hair and long black sideburns suggested that he could be of Latin extraction.

Judge Quinton whipped the picture from the table and savagely shredded it to pieces.

"There are certain magazines that would pay a small fortune for a set of photos showing the daughter of an eminent judge sowing her oats in such a prodigal fashion," our masked assailant said. "We have plenty more similar pics where that one came from — not only of your younger daughter but of the older girl, here . . . " He jerked a thumb in Judy's direction. "Perhaps she would like a set for the family album," he sneered.

Judy, wide-eyed, looked uncomprehendingly from the masked stranger to her step-father.

"That may — just may — have been my youngest daughter who somehow was tricked into being subjected to those disgusting photographs," said the Judge, harshly. "But don't dare associate my daughter here, with such filth."

"I'm not so sure about that, your honour," replied the other, mockingly. "Take a look at this one," and producing another photograph he flicked it with the same skill to land on the table before us.

It alighted face up, this time much closer to where I sat than to the Judge. There was no mistaking the fact that this picture portrayed two girls, dead-ringers for Janet and Judy, compromisingly disporting themselves with the same Latin gentleman watching them. Within seconds, this photograph shared the same fate as the first. Having savaged it to pieces it became obvious that it was touch and go whether the Judge would let his temper over-ride the menace of those twin-barrels pointing in our direction and hurl himself upon the two masked intruders.

"Take it easy, sir," I murmured soothingly, mindful of the spreading power of shot-gun pellets, even at this range. "Those photographs may well be fakes."

"Not a chance of that," replied the talkative one, curtly. Sensing trouble from the Judge he quickly transferred his weapon to his right hand again. "I assure you that not only will they be published, but copies of them will be posted to all the right people — unless we get what we came for."

"You've surely realised that Judge Quinton hasn't the faintest notion what it is that you are demanding.

Be reasonable," I chimed in, deciding that it was time I took part in the conversation if only to allow my host time to lower his blood-pressure. "Whatever it is that you're after isn't here in the house, therefore it's impossible to get it for you immediately."

"Then we'll take the girl along as hostage."

"Oh, no you won't!" cried Judy, suddenly twisting in her captor's somewhat relaxed grip and bringing one knee up sharply, in a most unladylike way, to sink into his groin, at the same time clawing at his masked face.

"You friggin' little Sheila!" roared her assailant, both hands pulling the stockinette hood back into position, what time his body bent nearly double as he took up the strain of that wicked knee-thrust.

The strong Aussie accent, plus a fleeting glimpse of a thickened malformed ear that was more scarred gristle than natural orifice, made me certain that this was Jimmy Luckin's chauffeur. Meanwhile, freed from his grasp, Judy beat a hasty retreat to my side of the table.

"Shall I go get her, sport?" asked the big fellow, one huge paw gently caressing that part of his anatomy that Judy's knee had so seriously disturbed.

The twin muzzles of the shot-gun, held rock-steady, now menaced the three of us. The recent little fracas must have caused his trigger-finger to itch, but since he had manfully refrained from turning us into human colanders I assumed that our destruction would only be forced upon him as a matter of dire necessity.

"No, leave her," he said, at last. "I'll come to a very simple arrangement with you, Judge. I'll telephone you sometime during the next two or three days. By then you should have the packet that I require and I'll give you instructions how it may be passed to us. Failing that, the photographs will be published — and, who knows, you may well lose your other daughter."

Lips clamped close, Judy's step-father eyed the other with a frosty stare.

"Well, yes or no?" the armed stranger demanded.

"Why should I bargain with scum like you?" the old man demanded. "What's in this packet that I'm supposed to hand over so freely to you?"

"There's no need for you to know what the packet contains. On no account must you open it. We know that it has been sealed and addressed to you personally. Best for all concerned if you arrange for it to be handed over to us — its rightful owners, I assure you. With that in our possession you will have nothing further to fear from us."

"How about prints of those photographs — and any negs you may have?" I asked.

"They will be handed over to you directly we receive the packet."

I looked across to my host. "It's up to you, sir, but if you'd like this arrangement to go ahead I don't mind acting as some sort of go-between when the packet and the photographs are due to change hands."

"I appreciate your offer," said the Judge, heavily, "But I'll have to sleep on this before I decide what action to take."

"OK. Just don't sleep too soundly," said the shot-gun gentleman, and then in an aside to his companion. "Can you think of any way to show them that we mean business? I've got them covered."

"My pleasure, sport," said his beefy friend. And then moving with remarkable speed for one so heavily built, he reached out a swift hand across the table and with one vicious wrench tore both blouse and brassiere from Judy, leaving her slim torso and beautiful young breasts fully exposed.

"That's for kneeing me in the balls, lady," he grinned. "If your old man don't come across with what the boss-man wants, we'll pick you up, an' I'll really enjoy you before I'm through, and that's a personal promise. But there, having seen those photos, I figure you'd be the one to enjoy that sort of exercise."

"All right, Ed," put in his companion, the name slipping out unnoticed. "Leave it at that. I'm certain they've got the message by now, so we'll be on our way. Best be sensible about this, Judge. And now, if anyone so much as takes a peek outa the front door or windows until we're well away, I'll use both of these barrels on them."

"Such extravagance!" I couldn't help saying as the pair backed off until finally we heard the front door slam.

No sooner had the door closed on them than I took the stairs in giant strides and peered cautiously from a front bedroom window. But quick though I'd been, their vehicle was already disappearing round a bend in the drive. I just had sight of a heavily mud-spattered rear number-plate that was quite indecipherable, before they vanished from view behind the high stone wall which skirted the grounds. At the sound of movement behind me, I swung round. Judy stood there, clutching her torn blouse decorously in front of her.

"This is my bedroom," she said rather primly. "I need to change."

"Of course," I said. As I left her and descended the stairs I fell to wondering how a girl such as Judy came to be the subject of porno stills.

"What are you going to do?" I asked, seeing my host making ineffectual attempts to use a telephone that had obviously been sabotaged.

"Fight them!" he bit out the words. "I'll not allow myself to be blackmailed in such an outrageous manner."

"And Judy?"

He relapsed into troubled thought. "I'll make arrangements for her to holiday well away from here," he said at last.

"And if they trace her?"

A troubled look appeared on his thin

features. "Do you — do you think they could?"

"I wouldn't put it beyond them."

"But I'm on the judiciary of this country. For years my whole life has been bent on upholding law and order. How can I give in to them?"

"How about your daughter's well-being, or indeed, possibly her life?"

"What's all this about my well-being and my life?" demanded Judy, now wearing a white heavy-silk blouse as she rejoined us. And then, as we both fell silent, she added with some heat, "I never saw either of those photographs, but if they were what I imagine them to have been, I was certainly not featured in them."

Mr. Justice Quinton and I exchanged glances. We had both seen the prints. There could be no mistaking the two girls who had been portrayed in the second photo that the intruder had flicked on the table before us.

"Judy, I think it would be best if you took a holiday well away from here for a few weeks," the old Judge said.

"Sorry, no can do," she replied firmly. "I've an exhibition of my miniatures due in Cheltenham soon. There's too much to be seen to — so, no holidays for the moment. I'm not afraid of the threats that those two made."

I looked across to where her stepfather stood in front of the wide stone hearth. Judy may not be worried, but he assuredly was!

8

THERE had been a long embarrassing silence before I finally took leave of Judy and her step-father. I politely refused the girl's offer to drive me back to the Hotel, for I needed to think and often had my most inspired thoughts while walking. Today, however, inspiration refused to materialise. Still wondering how best I could help Judy and the old Judge, I called in at the Hotel Bellevue to check that there were no messages for me. Then, having freshened up, I decided that a spin out towards Cirencester might prove an unexciting way of passing the rest of the afternoon.

For once, time was not of the essence, so I disregarded the comparatively straight run through on the A429, dawdling instead through Pinkwell and Calmsden, revelling in the almost complete absence of traffic on those winding, leafy lanes, allowing my MG to spin along at a modest, scene-enjoying pace.

Once I had reached Cirencester, traffic became a problem. In a way, I suppose, the Romans can be blamed for some of the town's congestion. Three of their highways — Akeman Street, Ermin Street and The Fosse Way — all entered the old Roman town of Corinium. True, the ring road now encircling the town relieves the narrow streets of much through traffic, but I have always found it best to explore Cirencester on foot. Since this afternoon seemed an exceptionally busy time for the old Town I heaved anchor at a relatively quiet parking place near the Abbey grounds, then took an enjoyable walk through the grounds themselves, leaving the path to take the longer route skirting the lake, until I finally passed the rear of the imposing parish church and emerged on to the Market Place. The reason for the build-up of traffic was immediately obvious. I had forgotten that it was market day.

Now, handed down on the distaff side of the O'Hara clan, I'm sure, is an interest in country markets. In fact I'm a sucker for them. It's not so much the bargains — although judicious shopping will often ensure that your cash pulls its full weight — but because of the interesting characters one sees there. A leisurely stroll round the colourful stalls convinced me that my wardrobe would be greatly enhanced by the addition of a light cashmere pullover at a price that was probably less than half the amount a London store would charge — or so I kidded myself!

Just then, chimes from the church clock reminded me that it was 4.30 p.m., while a faint empty gurgling let it be known that a little light sustenance would provide my ever-demanding digestive system with the work it was craving. Leaving the Market Place, I betook myself, smartish-like by narrow back doubles to a certain olde worlde tea-shoppe, where they put on a particularly satisfying line in Cotswold cream-teas. I have never been much of a gourmet, being very much in agreement with old Judge Quinton with his preference for plain, home-cooked grub, but many trips to this part of the country had made me something of a connoisseur so far as cream teas and ploughman's lunches are concerned. In the past I had found the cream teas of this particular establishment well up to expectations, being extremely free-handed with the butter, cream and strawberry jam accompanying warm, home-baked scones. Within a matter of minutes, the smiling, auburn-haired young waitress had placed before me my full measure of calories.

A peaceful fifteen or twenty minutes elapsed. I was busily piling the last of my ration of cream and jam on to the remaining morsel of scone when three boisterously noisy young fellows in their early twenties clumped into the tea-shop and with some profanity finally seated themselves at a nearby table. They were a tough-looking trio with their near aboriginal hair-styles and extravagant fashion in clothes.

Their spokesman, a tow-headed rough-neck with a deep white cicatrice scarring his lower left cheek, twisting that corner of his mouth into a perpetual sneer, snapped his fingers in the direction of the young waitress.

"C'mon, Ginger, let's be 'aving yer!"

"Yes, sir?" said the girl, arriving at their table but keeping a good arms-length distance from them.

"My mates and me want a large, strong pot o' tea," he said, leaning back expansively in his chair.

"Anything to eat, sir?"

"Naw, just fetch us the char!"

As she departed to see to his order, the tow-headed toughie leeringly watched the smooth movement of her nicely rounded haunches.

"Bet you'd like to lay that 'un, Ernie,"

observed one of his companions, daintily fingering a pendulous gold ear-ring that hung from the lobe of his left ear.

"I might just get around to that," boasted the tow-headed one.

"Garn, she wouldn't give you a second look."

"Oh, yes she would — if only to see who was havin' it off with 'er. What d'you think of that red-haired bit o' skirt, Willie?" he asked the third member of the trio, who sat slumped in his chair, his head cradled in his hands.

"Cripes, you asleep or summat, Willie? I said how d'you fancy that bit o' crumpet that just took our order?"

"Aw, lay off me, Ernie. I got a real low on. I need a friggin' shot real bad."

"I've got a little somethin' that'll help you along, Willie. Mind you, it'll cost. Shall we say a coupla quid?" With which, comrade Ernie, slipped one hand inside the garishly decorated black leather jacket he was wearing and brought forth a small white paper packet which he passed carefully to Willie.

"Go on, sniff that," he whispered. "It'll get your back up in seconds, mate."

His companion raised his head and looked at the offering with lack-lustre eyes. "This summat new?" he demanded. "Not sure I want this. A meth-pill would do for the time being."

"Go on, Willie, don't be so chicken. Sniff that and it'll put new life into you. I swiped some from the firm, yesterday. Thought I might flog it for a few quid at the fair-ground over the weekend. Take my word for it, Speedy Gonzales has got nothing on this stuff. Sniffed some myself this morning an' it blew my hangover in seconds. Don't 'arf make you feel randy, though."

"All right, thanks, Ernie," replied his companion, carefully opening the small packet and gingerly sniffing its contents, first with one nostril and then the other.

"Like I said, you owe me now. I took a bloody great risk in getting' it."

"Can you swipe any more?" demanded the ear-ringed member of the trio. "Look at the way it's made young Willie perk up. It's shore put lead in his pencil in double-quick time. How about cutting me in? I'll help you flog the stuff."

Before answering, the tow-headed one glanced cautiously around, saw that I was closer than he had realised, and said, "I'll see you about it later. Hold on, now, 'ere comes our char."

As the young waitress drew near, Willie, who certainly had taken on a new lease of life — nudged his companion suggestively. "Kin see what you mean, Ernie. She's a right little darlin'."

"My mates reckon you fancy me, kiddo," said Ernie, as the girl reached them. "How about us gettin' together some time?" And as she leaned over to place the tray of tea-things on the table, he cupped one full young breast in his beringed hand.

With a startled exclamation, the waitress straightened hurriedly and knocked his hand aside, whereupon he slid it up her skirt.

At this point I was about to take some action, myself, but the girl was equal to the occasion. Whipping up the jug of hot water that flanked the teapot, she poured a good measure into her tormentor's lap.

"Oh dear! So sorry, sir!" she said, and beat a hasty but dignified retreat to the rear of the shop.

For several moments the language from Ernie was just about as blue as it can come. Two elderly folk sitting by the window, paid their bill and hastily departed. The rather straight-laced lady behind the cash-till reached for the telephone, took the receiver off its rest, and stood with finger poised over the dial.

"No need to pay for the tea," she

said, icily. "Leave quietly this minute, or I call the police."

"Aw, c'mon, Ernie," said Ear-ring. "Y'know I can't afford to get on the wrong side of the filth for a coupla months or so. Let's beat it."

The tow-headed one rose to his feet, the scar that twisted one corner of his mouth, standing out white against his temper-inflamed cheeks. "I'll get that little bitch!" he stormed. "She'll be sorry she was ever born a woman by the time I've finished with her!"

As the shop-door slammed behind them, the older woman, whom I took to be the proprietress, crossed to the window and twitched the net curtain slightly to one side as she peered out after the departing trio.

"They haven't gone very far, Mary," she warned. "They're standing on the corner of the street. Do they know you're due to leave in a few minutes' time, I wonder?"

"I've never seen them before, Mrs. Carter," replied the young waitress. "I don't think they can know what my hours are, but if you don't mind I'll stay on until they've gone." She shivered. "They're horrible, aren't they?"

"Some of the young people today," said the proprietress, raising her eyes heavenwards. "Of *course*, you can wait here until you think it's safe to go home, Mary. I haven't seen them around here before. Shouldn't be surprised if they're not connected with that large fun-fair they're just about to open on Watermill Field outside the town."

I poured my last cup of tea and looked across to the two women.

"I'll be happy to escort the young lady home," I ventured.

"Thank you, sir, but I couldn't bother you so," replied the young waitress, eyeing me with the suspicion that was no doubt a carry-over from her mother's warning not to accept sweets from strange men.

"Nonsense, Mary!" put in the older woman. "I'll be a lot easier in my mind if you'll accept the gentleman's kind offer."

"Very well, thank you," said the girl. "I've a little clearing up to do. Perhaps by then those fellows will have moved off."

A thought suddenly occurred to me. When her young helper had disappeared to some nether regions I asked the proprietress what her normal closing time was.

"Five o'clock on week-days."

"Are opening and closing times shown on the door?"

"Why, yes, there's a small handwritten notice there."

"So that bright bunch will more or less know when the girl is due to leave. Always assuming that they can read."

"Of course, I hadn't thought of that. I'm more than ever glad that you've agreed to accompany Mary home."

The church clock was chiming five thirty when the girl and I were crossing the market place in the direction of the Abbey grounds. Fortunately, there was no sign of the three young hoodlums who had disturbed the tail-end of my cream tea. Now what had promised to be a fine June evening had changed with all the fickleness of our English weather. Canvas roofings flapped noisily in the growing wind as the last of the market traders dismantled their stalls, and the few late shoppers scurried away, all hell-bent on getting home before the heavy rain that the dark, lowering clouds were promising.

"You're in a hurry, man," came a familiar voice as we were passing the south porch of the church, with its battlemented parapet and fine bay windows.

It was young Andy, carrying a well-filled shopping-bag.

"This is Mary, a — er — young friend I'm just seeing home. Mary, this is Andy, another young friend of mine."

The two youngsters sized each other up and seemed to like what they saw. Introductions over, Andy gave me what my dear old Mum calls 'an old-fashioned look.' I hastily explained my reason for accompanying the girl, hopefully dispelling any notion he may have had regarding an ulterior motive for my unaccustomedly quixotic action.

"If you're going through the Abbey grounds I'll tag along with you," he offered. "Is that the shortest way home for you, Mary?"

She nodded. "It's normally a pleasant walk — but I'm not certain about it today," she smiled, buttoning a cardigan over her light summer frock as a gust of unseasonably chill wind reached out its fingers for us as we rounded the rear of the Church and faced the broad expanse of parkland beyond.

"Been on a shopping spree, Andy?" I asked, indicating the shopping bag.

"Grub and greens for the weekend," he grinned. "Leave your shopping until the market's on the point of closing and some things — especially the perishables — come a lot cheaper."

Mary shot him a shy, approving glance. Obviously such frugality appealed to her.

With the girl walking between us, we stepped out along the well-kept path which wound its way around the south-eastern edge of the Abbey grounds, quickening our pace as the first large drops of rain spattered down. The path snaked its way past various clumps of tree and bush, offering us some protection from the buffeting wind and strengthening shower, until we finally halted where the bosky wind-break ended. By now the downpour was beginning to assume monsoon proportions and since the remainder of our mini-safari needs must take us along by the side of the lake with practically no protection from the weather, we sought the shelter of a wide-spread, generously leafed chestnut tree, huddling close together against its aged bole. It was at that moment that we heard the sound of booted feet pounding along the macadam path towards us and rounding a corner came the three young toughs who had caused trouble in the tea-shop.

"Watch out, Andy," I warned. "They're the same three boyos that I mentioned earlier."

Without a word, he placed his shopping-bag at the girl's feet and took a pace forward so that he shielded her. He was too late. Leather-clad Ernie and his two buddies halted there in the pouring rain.

"Yer right! It's 'er alright," said the ear-ringed young tough, whose name I didn't know.

"Yeah, I kin see. Look, this bleedin' place is deserted now. If we see the bearded bloke an' that young spade off we can 'ave the girl, turn and turn about, rain or no friggin' rain."

"You mean, 'ave a little gang-bang, Ernie?" said Willie. "Cor, I really fancy that. Ain't never 'ad it in the rain before," and with this he took a shiny brass knuckle-duster from a jacket pocket and slipped it in an uncomfortably workmanlike manner over the fingers of his left hand.

'So, our Willie's a southpaw', I thought, and then watched as Ernie pulled a black-handled knife from an inside pocket of his leather jacket and flicked open a lean stiletto-blade, while Ear-ring uncoiled a length of cycle-chain from his waist and wound one end of it around his right hand.

"No matter what happens, Mary," I said, "you stay out of this. Should things look a bit dicey for us, run down there over that small bridge by the overflow from the lake. If you've time, knock at the first door."

"They're closing in, guv," said Andy.

"You take the one with the knuckle-duster. Watch it, he's left-handed, I think. I'll take the other two."

There was no time for further words. Coming forward in a half-circle, the three were on to us like the animals that they were. The thug with the cycle-chain swung it flail-like at my face. Ducking beneath it, I sank a left, right and left again into the softly sagging tissue of his midriff. With the breath expelled from him like a bursting balloon, he dropped first to his knees and as my foot took him on the jaw, slumped face down on the sodden grass.

Meantime, Ernie had circled to one side of me and came in fast. I saw the glint of the flick-knife and twisted aside just in time to avoid being punctured. I had only a second's respite, however, before the tow-headed young tough was after me again. He was proving a hard, well-muscled adversary who was obviously no stranger to the odd brawl or so.

I caught a momentary glimpse of Mary, white faced and eyes widely staring, before I was forced to concentrate on the matter in hand.

"Just stand still, you bastard," enjoined Ernie, "and I'll gut you like a fish!"

"Fresh herring or mackerel?" I asked, skipping nimbly aside to avoid a lunge that would certainly have started the filleting process just below my floating ribs.

"You're a clever sod, but I'll get you yet," he sneered, "An' then I'll have that little tart until she screams for mercy," and so saying he made another vicious under-arm jab at my anatomy.

This time, however, mounting rage and frustration had made him lose his cool. Expecting me to move out of reach again, he miscalculated and lost balance. I closed in swiftly. A well-placed kick of my leather-shod toes came into forcible contact with the humerus above his right elbow. The knife fell from his nerveless fingers. Moving closer in, my left fist sank into his solar-plexus and the blade of my right hand chopped unmercifully into the side of his throat. With a horrible choking sound he dropped as though he had been pole-axed, and lay writhing at my feet.

Turning, I was in time to see Andy feint with his left and deliver a right-cross to the point of Willie's neanderthal jaw with such force that I felt sure it would be many a mealtime before that young thug would be enjoying his food, unless he took his sustenance through a straw.

Just then, Ear-ring came wheezingly to his feet, saw his two companions the worse for wear, recumbent on the ground, and took off with a remarkable turn of speed for someone whose breathing had so recently been seriously interfered with. Seconds later he was followed by Willie, encouraged on his way by a nicely-placed foot from Andy.

"How about that one? He's out cold," said Andy, wiping the blood from a gash high on his dark cheek and indicating Ernie, who lay in a pool of rain as though he had just been scuttled.

"Leave him. He's breathing quite regularly now. With any luck, if he gets wet enough his joints will seize up with rust," I said, unfeelingly.

"I think I'll put these out of harm's way," said Andy, scooping up the bicycle chain, the knuckle-duster and the flick-knife. Crossing to the edge of the lake he hurled the assorted weapons far out towards the centre of the rain-dappled water.

"Are you all right, Andy?" asked Mary, solicitously, as he rejoined us. "Your cheek is bleeding badly."

"That's the rain washing the blood down my cheek," he grinned. "He caught me a glancing blow with that set of brass-knuckles he was wearing." Then turning to me, "Man, that was one hell of a nice scrap, wasn't it, guv?"

"There was a moment or two that I enjoyed," I was forced to admit.

"That cut on your cheek needs attention," put in the girl. "Look, we can't get much damper than we are already. I've a small furnished flat just on the other side of the Abbey grounds. Let's not wait around any longer. Once there I can clean up the cut and give you a cup of tea or coffee."

"Does the invitation include me?" I asked.

"Of course," she said, turning grave blue eyes momentarily in my direction before giving her full attention to Andy again.

'What it is to be young', I thought. Obviously, our comely young waitress had decided that I was old enough and ugly enough to take care of myself. And then I remembered Judy Quinton and in a much happier frame of mind trudged on through that over-moist June evening behind the two youngsters. Maybe, just maybe, I thought, we mature folk could get something going for us!

9

MARY'S flat proved to be minute rather than just small. No self-respecting cat would have chanced being swung around in the living-cum-dining room. At her invitation I seated myself on the single dining-chair while Andy was allowed to lord it in the sagging armchair by the gas-fire. Having passed each of us a towel, she took off her sodden cardigan and then busied herself in the enlarged cupboard which I took to be her kitchen.

Minutes later she produced three steaming mugs of coffee, plus cottonwool and antiseptic with which she proceeded to attend to Andy's gashed cheek. There was no doubt that Andy was well and truly smitten. His expressive brown eyes followed the girl's every move with all the dumb eloquence of a doting Spaniel. I decided that it would be most unsporting of me to play 'gooseberry', so quickly finishing my coffee I pleaded urgent business and made to leave.

Unspoken thanks from two pairs of eyes greeted my apology for having to depart them so soon. Ah, well, as we've heard so often, 'That's life!'

By now evening was setting in and although the rain had ceased it was still miserably damp — especially for Flaming June. I reasoned that a hot bath and stimulating drink were in order before dinner, and drove directly back to the Hotel. Later, while soaking my chassis in the comfort of hot water, during which time I sipped appreciatively at a whisky and ginger, I made plans for the evening.

Having arranged for the blazer and slacks I had been wearing that day to be cleaned and pressed, I changed into a sober suit — I'm really more of a casual dresser — and descended to the Hotel dining-room, where I made a simple but leisurely dinner of steak with trimmings, wine, a double go at the cheese-board (you're really a pig for cheese, O'Hara!) coffee and a liqueur. I then watched an American cops-and-robbers film on television — much more of a farce than the thriller it was supposed to be — and then returned to my room and changed into black polo-neck pullover, slacks and navy-blue wind-breaker jacket. Together with soft-soled shoes this completed my ensemble for the night.

It was still quite breezy when I slipped quietly out of the Hotel. A rising moon shone intermittently through scuds of dark cloud chasing each other across the scowling sky. With a large, rubber-sheathed torch dangling by its strap from my wrist — and this accompanying me as much for its truncheon-like quality as for the illumination it might afford — I stepped it out in the direction of Judge Quinton's place. I met no one on the road. The only signs of life were illuminated cottage windows, various squeaks and rustlings from hedge-rows and stone-walling, and, as I neared the end of my journey, the sound of a low-flying aircraft passing nor-west above me. The plane had no lights. I could just make out its shape, a small Cessna or similar craft, as it purred softly on its way some four or five-hundred feet overhead. Coming in to land? Possibly. Otherwise it was too low for safety.

"That you, guv?" came a whisper from the dark shadows of a wind-rustled covert.

"So you've made it, Andy. I wasn't sure whether you'd be able to tear yourself away from Mary."

I glimpsed the flash of his teeth. "Only managed it with difficulty. Say, man, isn't she a cracker? What's more she doesn't mind my skin being a delicate shade of milk-chocolate. Reckons my blood's as red as hers. Given the chance, though, I think she'd try to boss me around just like my old mum did."

"Just let her *think* she's bossing you around and there you have the recipe for a happy life — in or out of marriage," I said, then glancing at the luminous dial of my wristwatch, I added, "Have you been here long? It's later than I thought — only twenty minutes off midnight."

"Only 'bout ten minutes. There's a break in the wall through this field. No trouble about getting into the Judge's grounds."

"After you then, old son," I said. "When we get inside you take up a position watching the front of the house. I'll move on round to the back."

"OK. Follow me, but tread easy. We have to go through a thick spread o' nettle."

"Nice for the goldfinches," I murmured, following gingerly in his wake.

Only two lights were showing in the house as we drew close. One, in a front upstairs room I judged to be from Judy's bedroom, the other, downstairs, could well be her step-father having a night-cap. Leaving Andy well-nigh invisibly placed beneath a willow whose feathery foliage drooped almost to the ground, I picked a cautious way to the rear of the house, finally taking up my position in a neat little gazebo, complete with hard-wood bench, from which I was afforded an excellent view across a wide expanse of lawn.

Apart from the occasional rustling of nocturnal nature out and about in its nightly quest for nourishment and conquest, there was no other break in the silence. I fell to musing over events since I had first discovered Janet Quinton's body. Truth to tell, I detested the waiting game. Tucked away in some confidential file in the Gnome's office I was sure that there were some pointedly pithy remarks anent my headstrong disposition. Not to worry. There were a fair number of villains who could also have passed critical comment on this side of my nature.

Like so many other stake-outs that it had been my lot to experience, this one looked as though it would be equally boring and abortive. Soon after 2 a.m. there came the drone of an aircraft passing overhead. Without lights, flying low but climbing. The moon was so heavily obscured by black cloud that a passing shadow, like some huge winged insect, was all that I could see. Another hour passed, and I was alerted by the crack of a breaking twig from among the shrubs at the edge of the lawn. With torch at the ready, I moved to the door of the gazebo, ears flapping like an African Jumbo's as I homed in on the faint sounds of approaching movement.

"Guv, guv, where are you?" came a whisper.

"Here, Andy," I said softly. "Any trouble?"

The youngster stepped into the shadowy interior of the summer-house. "Two, mebbe three of 'em have just shinned over the front wall and are making their way round to the other side of the house."

"Did you get a chance to see any of them properly?"

"No, too ruddy dark, man! But one's a real bulky guy. Could well be the ape who you said roughed up Miss Judy, this afternoon."

"These characters may be armed," I warned him. "If you want to sheer off home I'll not think any the worse of you. I'm hardly paying you danger money."

"If there's to be any action, I want some of it," he said simply. "As to them being armed — I've got my air-pistol with me. In poor light it can look very off-putting and since it's a repeater-job I can trigger off a fair number of pellets that might trouble some of 'em."

"OK, Andy. We'll work our way round to the other side of the house. Follow close behind me."

Moving as silently as possible through the shrubbery bordering the lawn, we moved around to where a large garage was a later addition to the original old building. Andy stopped me in my tracks by giving a tug at my jacket.

"There's one of 'em, over there by the corner."

Sure enough, I saw a dark, bulky figure step out from the full shadows cast by the main building and look aloft to the roof of the garage. And there, making their way along a stone parapet at the rear of the garage roof were two other figures. As Andy and I watched, the two reached a window at the side of the old house, paused for a moment while a catch was forced, and then disappeared into the darkness beyond.

"I guess the one on the ground is too heavy for any cat-burglary," whispered Andy. "What next, guv?"

"Somewhere, in the lane outside, probably tucked out of sight in a field-entrance, they'll have a vehicle of some sort. do you think you could immobilise it?"

"No sweat," my companion grinned. "But that's going to leave you on your Tod, man."

"Not to worry, old son, just try to nobble their vehicle."

"This I'm looking forward to," he assured me, gliding off through the shrubbery.

Just then, the rear door of the house swung silently open and the remaining member's bulky figure disappeared within. I allowed a full minute to elapse and then took a quick and crafty sprint across the lawn and slipped silently into the old house by the same rear door. Helped by a shaft of moonlight which pierced an uncurtained window, I found myself in a stone-flagged laundry-room that was probably the scullery of the original house. From there I entered a large kitchen with a floor area that would not have disgraced a complete modern flat. Memory told me that this probably gave on to the dining-room where the Judge had hosted me for lunch earlier that day. The creak of a floor-board on the other side of a partly-opened heavy oak door warned me that there was company inside the room.

I was quietly assessing my next move when the splintering sound of a door being forced open on the floor above, followed by a muffled scream, brought me into the dining-room with the speed of a favourite from trap five. Snapping my torch on I shone it full into the eyes of the brawny customer who sought to bar my passage. But the force of my entry had brought me too close to him. A sweep of his arm knocked the torch from my grip and although it still swung loosely from its strap at my wrist so that crazy shadows danced around the room, he was on to me before I could properly seize the torch again.

This had to be Eddie Moxon, the Aussie ape whom the Gnome had warned me about. With a complete disregard for the finesse of in-fighting he bore down on me with his full and greatly superior weight, clamped both of his thick arms about my trunk and proceeded to squeeze the living day-lights out of me. At least, I have no doubt that this was his intention, but with my ribs actually creaking under the strain and a blood-red mist beginning to fog my brain I just knew that this was no time for niceties. Throwing my head back as far as it would go in the limited movement allowed it, I crashed it forward — once, twice — butting him savagely in the face.

Now we O'Haras have hard skulls. The humble coconut has often been named in their description. Even I saw stars with the force of that dual contact. Eddie must have found the effect quite paralysing. A string of rude but mumbled words left a mouth that was also being used to eject some broken teeth.

"You Pommie bastard!" were among the kinder epithets. But as his grip about me relaxed, my groping fingers grasped the barrel of the torch and with a fine round-arm swing I brought it crashing down just above his left ear. What the blow did to his head I can only guess. It certainly deprived me of my make-shift truncheon for the force of the blow not only shattered the lens and bulb but also tore the strap loose from my wrist, allowing the wrecked torch to ricochet from the Aussie's cranium and hurtle off into the darkened depths of the room.

But give him his due, Eddie was made in a tough mould. With a bellow like a bull that has just been parted from his favourite cow, he came at me again. There was no doubt that he was so spitting mad that he was all set to use the three 'fs' against me; feet, fists and fangs — or what remained of the latter.

With eyes now accustomed to the gloom I slipped to one side as he charged me. Then, with a neat bit of ankle-trapping I sent him sprawling. The violence of his fall must have shaken the old house to its foundations, but he was still game to get me. Before he could completely scramble to his feet, however, I caught up one of the heavy oak dining-chairs and brought it forcibly down on his head and shoulders. Y'know there must be something special about antique chairs. How many times do we see one character on television wrap a chair round another's head. And does it seem to have any marked effect on the assaulted one? Never! Be he hero or villain of the piece, he usually shakes his head, comes to his feet, and bores straight back into battle. Not so with Eddie Moxon. That big lummox just keeled over on to his back and lay there snoring heavily.

Tenderly favouring the knife-scar at my ribs, which in no way had been improved by the Aussie's far from friendly hug, I moved around to get my bearings in the room, trying to avoid bumping into furniture on the way. There came a soft click and the room was suddenly ablaze with lights from the cut crystal chandelier overhead and from the matching wall-lights. By the far doorway stood a hooded figure with the dark muzzle of a Mauser automatic trained in my direction. Flanking him, a second hooded figure supported Judy Quinton, slumped in a semi-conscious position against him.

"Stay right where you are . . . A single move and I'll empty the magazine into your guts!" With which the Mauser was lowered slightly to cover that part of my chassis adorned by my belt buckle.

"Who are you, anyway?" came the muffled query from the character supporting Judy.

"An innocent bystander . . . just looking up old friends of the family," I offered.

"Not so innocent or so bloody harmless if you managed to put *him* out," he said, nodding in the direction of the recumbent Eddie. "You deserve a lesson to teach you to stay out of business that in no way concerns you.

Put a slug in his knee-cap," he advised his companion. "It'll slow him up and serve as a reminder for him to keep his nose out of other peoples' affairs."

The Mauser ominously lowered its aim from my belt-buckle. But at that moment there came the regular thudding that one associates with some unfortunate glissading down a staircase without benefit of ice-axe or alpenstock. While to lend further drama to the moment, Eddie Moxon levered his head from the carpet with a deep groan, and sat there blinking owlishly at us through the eye-holes of his stockinette balaclava.

The villain who held Judy glanced quickly over his shoulder. "Hell, the old man has fallen down the flaming stairs. You couldn't have pumped enough of that junk into him. Looks as though he's broken his bleeding neck."

For a few fleeting seconds the Mauser-man's attention wavered. I covered the distance between us with a leap that wouldn't have disgraced a gazelle and sent him sprawling backwards through the open doorway, at the same time cannoning heavily into Judy and his companion. Reflex action caused him to trigger off one shot which shattered a piece of porcelain on the far side of the room. Then I was on to him and had twisted his arm so savagely that he was forced to drop the weapon. I was stooping to retrieve the Mauser, indeed, had it in my hand, when Judy's semi-conscious body was pushed on top of me.

"C'mon! Get the hell out of here!" snapped the villain who had been holding Judy. With this, he swung a leg and booted me a good solid kick in my long-suffering rib-cage, dragged his Mauser-less companion to his feet, demanded of Eddie Moxon that he should haul his arse off the carpet, and within seconds I heard their feet kicking hell out of the chipped limestone drive as they headed for the road.

Judy moaned faintly as I twisted

free from her and hurried over to the window with the idea of helping the three of them on their way with the aid of the Mauser automatic. But the three were no longer in view. Hoping that Andy would have the good sense to refrain from tackling them himself, I turned back to minister to Judy, lifting her gently on to a settee. There was an unnatural flush to her cheeks and the sleepily hooded eyes with their dilated pupils told their own story. A drug of some sort had been administered and there was little I could do until the effect wore off.

I suddenly remembered the sounds we had heard of someone descending the stairs the hard way. Sure enough, I found Judge Quinton in a crumpled heap at the foot of the wide, curving staircase. I had no means of determining the full extent of his injuries, but his cervical vertebrae seemed to be intact and he was breathing regularly, while my fingers at his carotid artery assured me that his heart was sending the red stuff pulsing around at a fairly normal rate.

The telephone proved to be mute, no doubt external wires having been cut yet again. The police and a doctor would have to be called and mindful of the public telephone kiosk some hundred yards up the lane from the house, I left by a rear door and made a swift but circumspect trot through the shadows edging the drive until I reached the splendid wrought-iron gates that gave on to the outside world.

There was no sign of Andy. Taking up a position in the deep shadow cast by one of the wide stone gate-pillars, I circumspectly surveyed the lane to make sure that the three villains had departed this neck of the woods. Suddenly, I stiffened to the icy touch of a pistol muzzle nuzzling the back of my neck.

10

"JEEZE, I'm sorry, man! Didn't know it was you," came Andy's apologetic voice as the cold circle of steel was withdrawn from the nape of my neck, leaving only a rich crop of goose-pimples to mark its passing. Even the muzzle of an air-pistol can have a traumatic effect when you're quite expecting it to be the business end of something much more lethal.

"Did you see them?" I asked.

"I surely did. There were four of 'em all told, y'know. One of the blighters had been left behind. The driver, I guess. He was parked in a field-gate opening, as you suggested, farther along the lane."

"Did they get away?"

"'Fraid so. Because of that fourth geezer in the car I couldn't get under the bonnet to nobble the engine. I was just about thinking of heaving a ruddy great lump of best Cotswold dry-walling through the windscreen and into his lap when the other three came pelting up. I thought it favourite to duck out of sight then."

"Very wise," I assured him. "What sort of car were they using?"

"A Volvo estate — either black or dark blue — hard to tell in this light. But I left my mark on it."

"How did you manage that?"

"As they shot past me I pumped about half-a-dozen pellets into the nearside bodywork. I doubt whether they heard it hit the car, it was accelerating so loudly. They must have left a few quids' worth of tyre-rubber on the road the way those wheels were scrabbling at the grit."

"Well, I'm glad that you're OK, old son. They may have got away, but empty-handed."

"Are things all right back there?" He jerked a thumb back towards the house.

"Could be better, but would have been a darned sight worse if we hadn't turned up, this evening. The house 'phone's been cut again. Would you get in touch with the police from that kiosk? Tell them that the Judge has been injured and an ambulance will be necessary. They won't let any grass grow under their feet then."

Without another word, young Andy moved off smartly up the lane.

"By the way, tell the fuzz that it's important for them to get a message through to Inspector Marlow," I called. "Give them my name and say that I'll be waiting back here."

When I returned to the house, I found Judge Quinton just as I had left him, unconscious but breathing steadily. Judy was showing a little more animation. She was rambling on like a child talking in her sleep, with her eyes only half open.

I hunkered down beside her and tried without success to make some sense of her disjointed mumbling. After a few moments she seemed to become aware of my presence. With a sob she reached out and clung to me like a frightened young girl.

"Michael, Michael, please help me," she sobbed, nuzzling her tear-stained cheek into my neck.

But there was little I could do other than clamp my arms about her and murmur the soothing noises that one would normally use for a frightened child. That Judy was truly scared I would have wagered my last bent penny, yet almost within seconds her whole attitude changed. First she drew herself erect so that we were both holding each other at arms' length and then with a sigh of near ecstasy she cupped my face in her delicately fingered hands and pressed her soft lips passionately against mine.

At first I mistakenly thought this was just her simple way of saying 'thank you' for my avuncular embrace. But no, there was nothing simple, nor innocent about the way in which her warm lips and probing tongue began to tremble out their message to me.

I've never counted myself as being particularly bright when it comes to understanding the fair sex, but I could have sworn that this was a pretty hot come-on for Judy, at such short notice. Then I remembered the photographs that the first intruder had so contemptuously tossed on the table in front of the Judge and me ... Maybe, both she and her late sister had nympho-inclinations. And this latter speculation was further strengthened when she took both my hands and brought them down to cup her full young breasts.

I would have dearly liked to put this sudden show of sexual enthusiasm down to my irresistible male charm, but somehow this idea didn't gel. As she pressed her body to me, there was a growing loosening of inhibition that I felt sure was out of character. Mind you, at any other time I would have welcomed the chance to kiss and caress her, but now it would have been too much like taking advantage of a girl who'd had the odd gin or vodka too many. And that was it, of course! Whatever narcotic those hellions had used must be strongly aphrodisiac and now that the girl was regaining consciousness she was being subjected to its full effect. And so, incidentally, was I!

Detaching myself with some difficulty I left her hugging a cushion while I moved off into the kitchen and brewed a mug of strong coffee. Returning with this, I was feeding Judy sips of the dark brew while adroitly avoiding her wandering hands which now seemed intent on establishing my manhood, when I heard a car braking hurriedly on the drive outside. Imploring Judy to take care with the hot coffee, I hurried to the front door and was faced with Inspector Marlow, about three strides ahead of three uniformed stalwarts of the law — two flat-cap constables and one woman in the new, fetching headgear. As they entered the house I saw that one of the uniformed men and the woman both sported three stripes apiece. Following in their wake came young Andy.

"Hmph! More trouble and you're in on it, I see," was the Inspector's opening gambit. "Do you know this young man?" and he hooked a thumb in Andy's direction.

"A friend. He was good enough to 'phone while I attended to the Judge and his daughter."

"Are they hurt — badly?" he asked, shouldering past me and dropping to one knee where Judge Quinton lay at the foot of the stairs.

"I think both Judy and the old man were given a shot of dope. The girl's coming out of it, but as you can see, the Judge took a nasty tumble down the stairs. I'm not sure how badly he's hurt."

"Doctor Grant is bringing an ambulance over. Should be here any minute now," said the Inspector. "It's hard to say whether the Judge is badly concussed or simply knocked out from the effects of the drug and the fall downstairs. At any rate both pulse and breathing seem about normal."

"Judy Quinton's in here," I said, as Marlow clambered to his feet.

"How come you're always Johnny-on-the-spot?" he growled.

"They do say I'm a magnet for trouble."

"So I've heard from elsewhere. Just what did happen here tonight?"

I quickly filled him in on the night's events.

When we entered the dining room we found Judy dabbing at a coffee stain on her dressing gown with a dainty but most inadequate handkerchief. I was pleased to see that the mug was almost empty, presumably supped by Judy since the stain on her clothing was not all that wide-spread, and a little coffee, like a little blood, does seem to go a long way when not in its intended place. She now seemed to be in control of herself again. As the Inspector bent down to ask her how she felt I couldn't help grinning as I thought of his reaction if Judy so far forgot herself as to reach out for him and plant one of her passionate kisses on his stern lips.

"I feel much better now, Inspector," she assured him, and then catching sight of my grin, which felt wide enough to unseat both beard and moustache, her face flooded with a swift surge of colour.

Isn't it nice to see a modern miss who can still blush?

"Are you quite recovered from the effects of the drug they used on you, Miss Judy?" Inspector Marlow asked solicitously, misreading her suddenly heightened colour.

"Yes . . . yes, I'm feeling . . . normal again," she said, shooting me a reproving look. "How is my step-father? I saw them use a hypodermic syringe on him before they injected me."

"He's still unconscious from the

effects of the drug," replied Marlow, diplomatically. And then, as we heard the sound of another vehicle swinging into the front drive. "I expect that's the ambulance now, with Doctor Grant."

"I — I don't really need to go into hospital . . ."

"Better if you have a proper check-up, Miss Judy. No telling what sort of dope those villains were using."

"The Inspector's quite right," I chimed in. "Just supposing the stuff has some really long-term effects?"

The look she shot me vouched for her memory of her recent loss of inhibition. It was only the entrance of Dr. Grant that silenced her. The Doctor was looking somewhat less than his usual dapper self. Tousled, would be the word to describe his appearance. The emergency call had probably roused him from a warm and comfortable bed.

"Where did they inject you, Judy?" the doctor asked, coming to the girl's side and looking professionally at her still slightly dilated pupils.

"In my forearm, just below my right elbow, here," and she indicated a mark with a small area of bruising around it.

"Not very skilfully administered. They almost missed the vein . . ."

"I was struggling at the time."

"Did it render you unconscious?"

"It didn't put me out completely. Somehow it seemed to lift me outside my own body. I couldn't stand unaided, nor use my arms and legs, yet all the time I felt as though I was floating on air — and nothing really mattered except my own happiness."

"I suppose you might say that it broke down a few inhibitions," I put in, helpfully.

This she chose to ignore. "How about my step-father? Is he all right now? He appeared to lapse into unconsciousness within seconds of being injected. Did I hear someone say something about him having fallen downstairs? Yes, I'm sure that I can remember one of the masked men saying that."

"He's being taken into the ambulance now, Judy," said Dr. Grant. "He may be badly bruised but I don't believe he suffered any serious injury. Are you quite sure that you don't want to come along to the hospital with him?"

"No thanks, Stephen. I'm sure that I'll be quite all right now. And I know you'll take care of my step-father."

"Then I'll be on my way unless you want me for anything else, Inspector?"

"Nothing at the moment," Marlow replied. "Thanks for turning out so promptly. You'll be letting me know how the Judge gets on?"

Dr. Grant nodded his dark head. "And you, Judy, will let me know immediately if you have any worrying symptoms when the drug wears off?"

"Yes, Stephen, but I'm beginning to feel normal again."

"I'll see you later, then," said the Doctor, and a minute or two later we heard the sound of the ambulance pulling away down the drive.

Inspector Marlow now turned his full attention on me. "Could anything have been stolen?"

"Nothing from down here," I replied, "And I should think the two who were upstairs must have spent most of their time subduing Judge Quinton and Judy."

"And that Mauser?" he queried, pointing to the butt of the weapon that was clearly visible where I had it holstered in the rather shallow pocket of my wind-breaker.

Without a word I passed the automatic to him and watched while he received it by passing a ball-pen through the trigger-guard. "Did it belong to them?" he asked, and at my nod of assent, "With your finger-prints on it, by now?"

"'Fraid so. In the heat of the moment I had no time for the niceties of detection."

"Hmph! I'll just take a look around upstairs for myself. Have you found anything worthwhile, up there, Sergeant?" This latter to the accompanying lady member of the force — a comely lass, despite flat heels, a longish skirt and a near masculine jacket that did nothing for her bustline.

"No sir. Just signs of a struggle — overturned chair, splintered door-lock, and rumpled bed-clothes."

"Excuse me, sir," Andy chimed in. "If I'm not wanted for anything else, could I get off home?"

The Inspector eyed him speculatively for a second or two. "We may have to ask you to call into the station in a few days' time. Before you go, give your name and address to the Sergeant."

"Many thanks for your help, Andy," I said, as his particulars were being painlessly taken down in the lady sergeant's notebook. "Keep in touch."

"Man, I sure will," he grinned, and left us with a jaunty stride, hands plunged deep into the pockets of the voluminous coat he wore, more to camouflage the outline of the air-pistol he had concealed there than for the warmth they provided.

Half-an-hour later the Inspector and his entourage had departed and the advent of a typically English June dawn was being heralded by a heavy downpour of rain. So much for Flaming June again!

Since Marlow had departed I had studiously avoided Judy, choosing to absent myself from the dining-room under the pretence of washing up the mug which had held her coffee.

"It's raining heavily," she said, when I returned.

"Probably just what the roses need."

"Did you walk here from the hotel?"

"Yes. It was a fine night when I set out."

"Well, you can't return in this. You can spend the rest of the night here — what there is left of it — You'll be quite safe and unmolested," she added with a faint smile. "The effects of that drug seem to have completely worn off. I — I'm sorry if you found my behaviour a little off-putting."

"Not at all, not at all! Anytime," I assured her gallantly, and really meant it.

"There's a guest-room upstairs, in fact you can have the choice of three. You might as well try to get some sleep."

"Not to bother. The settee down here will do fine. If I can crash down here for a couple of hours I'll be a new man by morning — I hope!"

"Help yourself to a night-cap," she said, indicating bottles and glasses hospitably arranged on a fine Sheraton sideboard. Just before leaving me she added, "and thank you Michael, for being here tonight. That's the third time you've been in the right place at the right time so far as I'm concerned. You're getting to be quite a habit."

Deciding against a nightcap, for truth to tell I was feeling rather shattered and was quite sure that I'd need no soporific of any sort. I kicked off my shoes, and my last thought as I stretched out on the settee was what an improvement it would be if only my head was pillowed on Judy's breasts instead of the brace of cushions that were now serving me in that respect.

11

I MUST have really flaked out. It was turned nine-o'-clock the next morning before the aroma of coffee and the sound of sizzling bacon penetrated my subconscious. You can keep all your alarm-clocks, there's nothing like the promise of food to awaken an O'Hara. I roused to one elbow and unglued an eyelid as Judy placed a king-size mug of coffee that somehow looked out of place on the delicate little Sheraton table alongside my makeshift bed.

"Milked but not sugared. That is how you like it, Michael?"

"Thanks, you're a ministering angel," I said, swinging to a sitting position and cradling the mug in both hands. "Come to that, I'm darned if you don't look the part. How come, after the sort of night that we experienced, you still manage to turn up first thing in the morning looking like a — a — an advertisement for health salts?" I ended lamely.

"I'm not sure that I like the analogy," she laughed, "But if it's meant as a compliment, thanks. Breakfast in a few minutes. I don't suppose you have to shave," she said, eyeing my hirsute visage, "but if you'd like a few private moments, the main bathroom is the first door on the left at the head of the stairs. While you've gone I'll 'phone the hospital to see what sort of a night my step-father had. A telephone engineer was here really early repairing the line — Inspector Marlow bringing pressure to bear, I expect."

By the time I had rejoined her, Judy had set a full spanking breakfast before me. "How's the Judge," I asked, spearing a plump sausage.

"Badly shaken and bruised but no internal injuries. They're keeping him in hospital for another day or two, but I gathered from the ward sister that the enforced rest isn't pleasing him at all."

"It was a nasty fall for a man of his age."

"You could probably benefit from a little of the same treatment," she said.

"You mean that all this excitement is likely to be too much for someone of my age?" I grinned.

"Well, you didn't get off entirely scot-free. There are some deep lacerations on your forehead that I didn't notice before."

"I brushed and combed my hair, especially to have breakfast with you. As for my forehead — they're tooth-marks."

"Tooth-marks?"

"S'right," I agreed, and told her how I'd had to butt my way free from Eddie Moxon's bear-hug.

"Oh, that big ape," she shuddered. "Do you know him, then?"

"I've heard of him. I believe he's acting as the tame heavy for James Luckin. You remember him, the fellow whose face hurt your hand at the *Pig and Parsnip* a few nights ago?"

She nodded. "That was the man who tried to blackmail me with some photographs he said he had." She paused. "I never saw the photographs that you and my step-father were shown. Were they — really horrible?"

"Not the sort to be shown a doting maiden aunt, I'm afraid."

"Was, was poor Janet in the photographs?"

"One of the girls was Janet. There were actually two girls, disporting themselves rather basically."

"Do you know the other girl?"

I nodded gravely. "Look, Judy, I value your friendship but I must be frank about this. I'm not only capable of calling a spade a spade but also a bloody shovel a bloody shovel!"

"So?"

"I think the other girl in the photograph was you."

Judy's face suddenly blazed with colour. "You're mistaken. I'm no prude but I'd never let myself be photographed — like that!" she said vehemently.

"Would it have been possible for you to have taken any sort of drug? I don't know how clear your memory is of events yesterday as the effects of that injection that our visitors gave you took hold."

"I remember, but don't read anything too flattering into my reactions then. At the time I felt as though I was on cloud nine — or cloud cuckoo land," she said rather bitterly. "No, I've never taken any drugs like that before."

"Then let's leave the matter of those photographs for the time being. The police have things in hand and now that an eminent judge has been assaulted in this fashion I'm sure they'll make every effort to catch those responsible."

"And just where do you fit into all this?" she asked. "You say you're partly on holiday and partly on business. I wonder what your true business is?"

It was symptomatic of my strong regard for the girl that I broke my cover and told her all.

"I can understand this need to clamp down on drug-trafficking. I've read that addiction figures are escalating in a frightening manner. But why should your search be concentrated in this backwater of the Cotswolds?" she finally asked.

I shrugged. "We've had certain information and have to act upon it. At the moment I fail to understand why your family seems to be bearing the brunt of villainy; why your sister should have been murdered, the Judge threatened and assaulted, the threat of blackmail, and presumably this attempt to kidnap you."

"There was also the murder of that young man, Gary Warren," she said.

"A close friend of your sister's, I believe. Tell me, Judy, what was Janet really like?"

"She was always a rather harum-scarum kid. As the younger child, she was rather spoiled, I suppose. As she got older some of her escapades were bringing my mother a lot of grief. Finally, when she was sent down from University — having become involved in a fairly sordid affair — she refused to return home, instead going to live in some sort of commune somewhere on the fringe of North London. It was not until Mother was killed in that riding accident that she returned home. But by then she was drinking heavily and, I'm fairly certain, taking drugs. I tried to make her see sense, if only for my step-father's sake, but she was a wilful girl."

"How about your step-brother? The Judge's son by his first marriage?"

"You mean Tony — Tony Quinton. I've never seen him and to my knowledge he's never been in touch with his father for years now," she paused. "As you must have realised, my stepfather keeps his feelings very much to himself, but from what little I've heard, he was really heart-broken over his son's behaviour."

"There are rumours that he's out

East somewhere now?"

"Perhaps. A typical black sheep, probably abroad, but just where I've no idea."

At that moment the telephone rang and cut into further conversation.

"It's Inspector Marlow," said Judy, offering me the 'phone. "Asking for you. I wonder how he knew that you were still here?"

"Using his crystal ball again. A regulation issue for ranking constabulary."

"What's that about a crystal ball?" came the Inspector's voice.

"Just making small talk with Judy," I replied. "Was there something?"

"Hmph! May be of interest. There was a minor gang fight last night at the fairground outside Cirencester. Some local lads got involved with a bunch of young thugs who seem to work evenings at the fair."

"Any serious injuries?"

"One local youngster received a stab wound that punctured a lung.

Fortunately, we were called in early and were in time to put a stop to most of the mayhem. But the thing that you might find of interest is that one of the fair-ground types that we pulled in — we think he was the one who inflicted the stab wound — was in possession of several small packets of dope. He'd been pushing the stuff, we understand."

"Wonder whether I know him," I said, and described the three characters who had set about Andy and me in the Abbey grounds. Without hesitation, Marlow pinpointed Ernie, the tow-headed tough with the scarred face, who had been the leading character in the attack that rainy afternoon.

"He's been through our hands before," said the Inspector. "Car theft and minor larceny. We're holding him on G.B.H. and drug-pushing charges. With luck he should be out of circulation for some time."

"Is he a local lad?"

"No, down from Brum. His normal

job is a van-driver with a health food firm. Seems to have been moonlighting with the fairground."

"More chances for him to push drugs to the youngsters," I suggested.

"Likely so. He's an unpleasant type. I hope the bench throw the book at him. It's a pity he can't come up before Mr. Justice Quinton. He'd get it really strongly then."

"This health food firm — is it near Bibury?"

"I believe it is. Why?"

"I know a youngster who needs a job. Sounds as though they may have a vacancy there."

"Could be worth a try. Shouldn't think a health food firm would want anything to do with anyone caught pushing drugs."

"Many thanks for the info," I said. "By the way, what sort of dope was he pushing?"

"Not certain. Something new — probably heroin-based — I'll let you know as soon as we've had it properly analysed," he paused and gave his usual little grunt. "Hmph! If you're down this way in the near future, look in. Might be able to spare time to take a jar of ale with you."

"Thanks. I'll hold you to that," I assured him.

As we both rang off I turned to Judy. "Could you spare time for a short run out to see that youngster I've had helping me?"

"You mean the young watch-dog you employed to make sure that I don't keep a clandestine appointment in the village, after dark," she smiled. "After all, the local milkman is rather dishy and there are rumours that he's quite free with his favours."

"You know darned well why I asked Andy to keep watch."

"Careful, it almost sounds as though you might care," she murmured.

"But I do. Can I show you?" I asked, closing in on her.

"You mentioned something about calling on Andy," she said rather breathlessly, as we both came up for air after an embrace that was not all one-sided, I'm pleased to say.

"Right. Can we go in your chariot?"

"If you mean Maudie, my Marina, yes!"

It was an extremely pleasant experience to be driving along the Cotswold byways with Judy as my companion. Once again I marvelled at the absence of traffic on the winding leafy lanes. Since we had lingered rather over breakfast, it was approaching eleven o'clock before we finally let go the anchor at a small stone-built homestead where Andy, in shirt-sleeves, was busy doing industrious things in the front garden. And surprise, surprise, Mary from the tea-shop was right there helping him.

"Would you like coffee or tea?" Mary asked, after introductions had been made. "Andy and I were just thinking of a mid-morning break."

While the two girls retired to the kitchen, I seized the chance to mention the possibility of a job to Andy.

"You can drive, I suppose, Andy?"

"Yes, my old banger is down there in the barn," he hooked a thumb towards a sizeable stone-built building behind the cottage. "It's legal, taxed and insured, but the cost of petrol has kept me off the road these past few weeks."

"I've got to admit that shanks' pony is a lot cheaper these days but rather more time-consuming. Would you like an advance on your watchdog wages so that you can run out to Bibury?"

"Thanks, no. You realize that if I land this job I may not be able to put in so many hours for you?"

"If you get the job you may still be working for me as well, old son. I've a notion that all's not strictly legit with that firm — just a suspicion mind you."

"I'll take it if it's offered, guv. Y'see, Mary an' me have something going for us. In fact, we want to get married as soon as possible. An' it can't be too early for me, man!"

"So soon?" I smiled.

"Yes, she's a cracker, isn't she?"

I looked across to the cottage where I could see Judy and Mary busily preparing our elevenses. "They're both crackers, old son," I said.

Just then a call from the girls summoned both of us inside. It was a cosy little home in the true sense of that word. Typical of so many of these stone-built Cotswold dwellings. Exposed beams and stone-faced chimney-breast with useful pinewood shelves set into each recess on both sides of the fireplace, caught the eye in the dining-room. I grinned to myself as I was shown further around the ground floor and mentally fell into estate-agent's jargon in summing up the cottage. It was good to see how much pride Andy took in the place.

"Mary's having to pay so much in rent for that crummy little flat of hers that we want to get spliced as soon as possible." And then probably aware of my unspoken query he added, "It's got to be all legal an' above board. If we have any youngsters of our own I don't want that they should have the same chip o' bastardy on their shoulders that I've got."

"You worry unnecessarily about that," I said quietly. "You're a man for all that." I paused to look at a rather faded photograph, framed in maple, which showed a young woman of level brow and handsome features.

"My mother when she was about twenty-four years old — a year before I was born," Andy said simply.

I glanced across to where Mary had paused in the act of buttering hot scones. Our eyes met in a knowledgeable glance. Words weren't necessary. She obviously knew about the chip on Andy's shoulders, and thought no less of him for it.

"I'm off to see about that job now," Andy said a little later, finishing the last crumb of home-baked scone. "There's just about enough petrol in the tank of my old banger to get me there and back."

"Good luck. Watch your step. Let me know how you get on," I said.

"I'll watch it, man, never fear," he said, and minutes later his beat-up old Ford Escort disappeared down the lane in a mild pall of blue exhaust smoke.

"Those two don't need any matchmaker," observed Judy with a smile, as we drove down the lane ourselves some twenty minutes later.

"Ah, young love," I said. "Where would some of our novelists and songwriters be without it?"

"Oh, you're the cynical one," she smiled, moving up through the gears as the lane straightened out in front of us.

Conscious of that firm young thigh so close to mine in the confined front seats of her small saloon car, I thought that love, young or otherwise, had much to commend it. Certainly, this scion of the O'Hara clan was beginning seriously to consider relinquishing a fancy-and foot-free existence.

12

WE stopped off for lunch — a simple Ploughman's Platter — at the *Pig and Parsnip* and it was well on into the afternoon when Judy dropped me off at the Bellevue. Having taken my leave of the girl in warm, time-honoured fashion, I turned and was about to make my way into the Hotel when I caught sight of a spanking new Rover 3.5 litre lording it in a corner of the forecourt. I recognised the vehicle and knew that I had a visitor — Sir Norman Norrick in person again, no less.

He was waiting for me in the lounge. "Anything to report, m'boy?" was his first greeting.

"Nothing that's likely to set the Thames on fire, at the moment."

"Well, let's get up to your room. You can order tea to be sent up — best

Darjeeling and they might as well send along a selection of pastries. This Cotswold air makes you feel damned peckish."

When wasn't he ever, I thought, placing the order for tea and following his diminutive figure across to the lift. How one person could have such a staggeringly high intake of calories and remain dwarf-size, I'll never know.

"Not much progress made since you've been here, O'Hara," he said as I closed the room door behind us. "In fact, let's face it, you've achieved bugger-all!"

"If I was to act only when I receive leads from your desk-bound department there might be some justification for censure. Here, look at these toothmarks. They weren't caused by a low-flying set of dentures," and I launched into a brief account of happenings since last he had called here at the Bellevue.

"Yes, yes!" he said testily. "But you're no nearer discovering if this new heroin-based dope is being made up and distributed from around here. And if it bloody well is, just who're busy ripping off a fortune from this particular connection."

As usual my irascible little boss was expecting miracles without admitting that a modicum of time was necessary before the average bloke could achieve them.

"Have *you* anything new to offer?" I asked pointedly.

"Well, on the overall picture we know that gang warfare plus stricter governmental controls in the Golden Triangle — North Burma, Laos, Thailand and the Yunnan Province has cut the opium output considerably, with the result that there has been a lowering of the opium-heroin trade passing through Hong Kong. The price of heroin has started to escalate so that traffickers are finding it necessary to dilute their dope with caffeine, codeine or similar muck."

"And is this the new Mega-H stuff

that we're chasing?" I asked.

"Not by a bloody long chalk! The diluted dope has far less of a murderously strong addictive power compared to Mega-H. I've seen some of it. Duclos sent some across from Paris. It's off-white in colour — a pale pinkish, biscuit colour."

"Do we know the additive they're using with the heroin?"

"All the analysts have been able to come up with is that, they think, it's of vegetable origin. But then so's bloody heroin, itself, dammit!" He paused, and added thoughtfully. "Some of the results of addiction to this new stuff are too hairy for words. There must be thousands of stupid buggers already wrecking their lives with the muck and if we don't scotch things it's going to provide one hell of a headache for Western civilization. Mega-H is a real destroyer."

There was a knock at the door and Millie Gray, the apple-cheeked waitress brought in a tray of tea and pastries and set them down on the table before us.

"That's very nice of you m'dear," remarked my diminutive boss, seizing upon one chocolate eclair that fairly filled his small fist. "These look particularly good. Well, go on, Michael, m'boy, give the lady something for her trouble." And with this he took a careful bite at the end of the chocolate-coated pastry, and once his mouth was full succeeded in decorating a corner of his rosebud mouth with a generous blob of cream.

Thanking me nicely for the coins I passed her, little Millie left us alone again.

"You were asking if I had any new information," the Gnome said, finishing the eclair and immediately reaching out for a cherry-topped madeleine cake. "Well, I've nothing positive y'understand, but Archie Clay in the 'Scrubs' has squeaked some more." He paused and truncated the madeleine with a single healthy bite. Thereafter a few seconds elapsed for some spirited mastication while he rid his palate of desiccated coconut.

"As you know, Archie was well into a dope connection when we nailed him. He eventually appeared before Mr. Justice Quinton who, as is his wont with anyone found guilty of drug trafficking, really threw the book at him. At the time I remember how little Archie was shit-scared when he heard that Quinton was going to preside. He was heard to say that the Judge had even sent his own flesh and blood down for a stretch for coining it with illegal drugs. We didn't think much of it, at the time. Now, Archie maintains that Quinton actually sentenced his own son, although I've been unable to substantiate this by checking back through past records. However, when we leant on Archie a little more he swore that the old man really had jailed his own son."

"But a Judge would never preside over his own son's trial," I protested.

"In the normal way, of course not," said the Gnome, eyeing the plate of pastries rather longingly, but finally wiping his pink lips meticulously on a snowy-white handkerchief produced from the sleeve of his jacket. "But rumour has it, according to Archie, that some years ago a young fellow came up in front of Judge Quinton. Some plastic surgery necessitated by a gang-fight, plus an alias that held water throughout the trial, is thought to have misled the Judge into believing that he was dealing with a stranger, but towards the end of the trial when it was obvious that a verdict of guilty would be found, the young man made some carefully-chosen remark that alerted Quinton to the fact that he may be in judgment of his own kith and kin. However, if it had been the prisoner's idea of obtaining a lighter sentence he was sadly mistaken. When found guilty he was sent down for a five-year stretch."

"That's quite a story. Is it possible?" I asked.

Sir Norman shrugged. "Who knows, m'boy, more things in heaven and earth, and all that. However, following on this, I made a 'phone call or two and as far as I can discover, the character whom Judge Quinton sent down about that time could have been a young man called Bradbury. During his spell in gaol he proved such an exemplary prisoner that he was allowed to complete an external degree course in chemistry — at which he showed a considerable flair — at one of the redbrick universities. The coincidence is that before he left home and 'dropped out' Tony Quinton was also thought to have quite a future in chemistry."

"If he was such a model prisoner I suppose he received some remission of sentence?"

"That he did — the full whack!" agreed the Gnome.

"Do you know where he is now?"

"No, all I've been able to find out is that first he took off for Sydney in Australia, then had a spell in New

Guinea, he next surfaced in Hong Kong, and was last thought to be heading back to New Guinea again."

"Have you been on to Judge Quinton to see whether he'll admit to having sentenced his own son?"

"I tried a few days ago and met with some prevarication, I thought. Now the old bugger's in hospital after that fall downstairs. The latest news is that he may have suffered a mild stroke — his heart's rather dickie — so they're keeping him in. Must say I feel rather sorry for the old boy. I suppose most families have the odd skeleton rattling around in the cupboard, but if rumour is right, that would certainly be a nasty memory for a judge of his eminence."

"Strange how so much of the latest skulduggery seems to be centred round his family. Have you any further news about the murder of his daughter Janet, or Gary Warren?" I asked.

"Nothing new. At one time we could have been forgiven the notion that having killed the girl in some sort of a lovers' quarrel, Warren then killed himself. But the police medico poured cold water on that one — certainly so far as Warren's death is concerned. The state and position of the wound, plus the complete absence of weapon rules out suicide."

"Did he have any relatives? Wife? Parents?"

"Haven't been able to locate any. Though if he's left any sort of a will someone's going to strike it bloody rich."

"How come? University drop-out, hotel bar-tender. I thought he must have been something of a poverty-stricken nonentity."

"Far from it," said the Gnome brusquely. "We've discovered that not only was Warren a director of a health food firm but he also owned the Bellevue Hotel. A fact that Courtney Fisk, the Hotel manager, has only just seen fit to mention to the police. He was apparently sworn to secrecy about his ownership of the place when he took it over about a couple of years ago. The story was that he hoped to have something quietly put aside when his retirement came up."

"Not many youngsters of his age worry about their retirement," I said.

"That rather depends what he was expecting to retire from," replied the Gnome, cryptically.

"This health food set-up, is it a local firm?"

"Yes, somewhere out beyond Bibury, I believe."

"Well, there's one connection between Janet Quinton and Warren," I said. "She was also a director of that company."

Sir Norman tugged thoughtfully at his rather pendulous lower lip. "Very interesting, m'boy. A place that will bear looking into, don't you think?"

"Being attended to," I replied, and went on to tell him about young Andy Richards and the job he had gone after.

"Hm, I don't like bringing in

amateurs, especially young 'uns," he said.

"This one's all right. I'll vouch for him."

"And who's paying him?"

"I am. Cash in hand at the moment."

"Out of your own pocket, of course," said the Gnome, craftily.

"At the moment, yes, but all payments will be entered on my final expense account."

"Then I'll expect better results from you than I've had so far, if you expect your expenses to be met in full," he said. And coming to his feet he headed for the door, paused to give me a brief bird-like nod, and then left.

As though obedient to the dramatic needs of the moment, as the door closed on the Gnome my telephone rang.

"A call for you, Mister O'Hara," came the soft Gloucestershire accent of the young lady at the hotel switchboard. As I was connected with my caller I recognised the voice of Mrs. Martin, the likeable old widow who often rented me a small cottage here in Upper Chilworth.

"My last holiday tenants have just moved out, Michael," she said. "The place has been cleaned and dusted. It's all ready for you with fresh bedding and towels, and milk, butter and cheese in the fridge, and a cob of that nutty wholemeal bread that you like in the bin."

"I'll move in early this evening," I promised. "I suppose the key to the cottage is still in its usual hiding-place?"

"That's right, Michael, under the large flat stone by the potted geraniums."

"And that's your idea of security," I laughed. "One of these days we'll all be raped in our beds."

"Hope springs eternal," came the reply, with a surprisingly youthful sounding giggle from someone well into her seventies.

"For shame, Mrs. M. And you with three sons and two daughters spread around the Commonwealth," I said.

"Yes, I'm a shameless hussy," she admitted. "But I'll be here when you come this evening. No embroidery class at the village hall tonight, so call in for a chat and a mug of cocoa. I would have called in to see you at the Bellevue but the old rheumatics have been rather bad this past week. Don't think I could have managed to climb that hill to the hotel."

"Sorry to hear that the 'screws' have been playing up again. I'll bring a bottle of something with me to help oil the joints."

She giggled again. "That will be nice."

Poor old Mrs. Martin, I thought as I replaced the receiver. Apart from a small pension the rent from the cottage adjoining her own was the only other income she had. It must be a frugal, lonely life, although the village folk were always good to each other, with a warm neighbourly spirit in this straggling little village. But in bad weather, when heavy falls of snow could cut telephone and power lines for days on end, and make these narrow hilly lanes impassable for vehicles, I couldn't help thinking that it must be a rather bleak existence for an elderly person like herself. And then I remembered the view from her living-room window, and from the cottage next door, when for most of the year the valley lay green and bright below her. Maybe there were compensations for loneliness.

Later that day, having settled things at the Bellevue, I visited the old lady and, as promised, presented her with a bottle of 'Mother's ruin' — her favourite but temperate tipple. As I was consuming a wedge of home-made fruit pie, I brought up this question of her loneliness."

She gently smiled. "I've had so many happy days here, Michael," she murmured softly, looking around the over-furnished little room, with its wealth of bric-a-brac on mantel, shelves and window-ledges. "I may only have memories now, but they are good memories, all bound up in this cottage. Every one of these trinkets has a story and a memory for me. Some folk rely on photographs, songs or snatches of music to stir their memories, but I need these," and she indicated the many small treasures that occupied most flat surfaces of the room.

"Can I pay you a month's rent in advance?" I asked, later that evening, about to depart for the neighbouring cottage.

"Are you really here for four weeks, this time, Michael?" she said, her face flushed with pleasure. "I've no other bookings until the start of the school holidays when I'm expecting a headmaster and his wife. Usually you can't manage much longer than a fortnight."

I wasn't too sure that the Gnome would stand for me remaining in this part of the country for that length of time. Then I thought of Judy Quinton and cocked a metaphorical snook at my boss. To hell with the department's needs after this assignment. For the first time my private life was becoming of paramount importance.

"I'll be here for a full month," I assured her.

"And I'm sure that will be nice for all concerned — especially Miss Quinton."

"Now what's that supposed to mean?"

She cocked a bright and knowing eye at me. "This is really quite a small village although we're spread out around the valley. You'd be surprised how we gossip. Goodnight, Michael. She's a really lovely lass. Pleasant dreams," and she ushered me to the door and so out into the brilliant moonlight.

Having cleaned my teeth and performed the usual nightly ablutions before hitting the hay, I fell to wondering whether Andy had succeeded in securing the van-driver's job. If so, would he be able to manage his watchdog stint tonight? What with one thought and another, especially the thought of Judy being alone in that large house, instead of climbing into pyjamas — well, at least the bottom half of same — I donned dark slacks and my old golf jacket, let myself quietly out of the cottage and rubber-soled it sneakily down the front path until I was well out of earshot of Mrs. Martin's place, and then headed for Judge Quinton's mini-mansion with all the fervour of a tyke who's just remembered where he's buried a favourite bone.

13

IT was well past the witching hour as I trod the now familiar lane that led down into Lower Chilworth and across to the higher ground. It was a fair night, chilly for June perhaps, but moon and stars were having their winsome way in a cloudless sky.

Andy saw me before I saw him.

"It's all right, guv, I'm here as usual," he said, stepping out from shadows cast by the Judge's front portal.

"How'd the interview go?" I asked, as we both eased back out of sight.

"Landed the job. The character who interviewed me — a coloured bloke, as it chanced — just asked me how I knew they were short-handed. Made up a yarn about having overheard something in a pub an' had come on to them straight away."

"Did you have much chance to look around?"

"I saw a workman-like looking packing and despatch department and a well-stocked warehouse. Didn't get a chance to case the office side of the firm, but they don't seem short of a quid or two. My vehicle's going to be a brand new Bedford van, with a smart looking paint-job on the sides."

"Do they manufacture or just distribute, do you know?"

"Prob'bly both. There are some sort of workrooms or lab'ratories to the rear of the place, but I was told there'd never be any call for me to go back there. My job would be to help load my van and then take in all the deliveries for Gloucestershire and Oxfordshire. There's another van — a long wheel-base job — that does the long distance trips. But man, that's a mint new vehicle as well."

"I'm glad you were offered the job, old son. When do you start?"

"Clocking-on at 8.30 tomorrow

morning. Don't worry, guv, I'll keep my eyes peeled and report back reg'larly. I rather fancy I saw a Volvo estate car tucked away in one of the open sheds that serve them as garages. It just might be the one I peppered with air-gun pellets the other night."

"Find out what you can, but take things easily. You may have found yourself a steady little job with a respectable firm."

"You don't really believe that, man."

"No, I must confess that I don't think the firm's as legit as it seems."

"One thought did occur to me."

"And that was?" I said.

"Those little packets and pill bottles that they knock out by the hundred thousand could be ideal for spreading around the odd batch of dope to interested parties."

"I've had the same suspicion, Andy. Now, since you've joined the ranks of the fully employed as from tomorrow, and we don't want you making a late start, nip off home. I'll hang on here for a while longer."

A minute or two later, resigned to a lone vigil, light suddenly streamed out as the front door opened, and Judy stood there silhouetted against the brilliantly-lit rectangle. Whatever night-attire she was wearing, it was quite translucent with that back-lighting. She was holding a tumbler in one hand.

"Malt whisky and water — would that be a suitable nightcap, Michael?"

"How did you know I was out here?"

"I've been expecting you. In fact, I've been watching out for you. Quite disappointed when Andrew turned up by himself. And there's a shameless confession."

"Shameless or not, I'm darned glad to see you. The nightcap is welcome, as well."

"Then come inside and enjoy it properly," she urged. "Do you think we're likely to have more company tonight?"

"I hope not."

"I suppose it was only that wonderful protective instinct of yours that brought you here."

"Something like that," I grinned, and as I sank a good third of the tumbler's contents in one smooth swallow, allowed myself the luxury of an appreciative look first at my attractive companion and then around this beautifully furnished room.

Catching sight of a silver-framed photograph of the Judge, his two stepdaughters and another fellow, whose face seemed vaguely familiar, I said, "Is that the Judge's son, Tony Quinton?"

"No, that's not Tony. But surely you know who it is? He's without a moustache there, of course. The photograph was taken several years ago when my Mother was still alive. In fact she was holding the camera at the time."

I took a closer look at the photograph. "Stephen Grant — Doctor Grant, as is?"

Judy nodded. "Yes. In those days he

was almost a member of the family. He was certainly much more Daddy's confidant than either Janet or I."

"I had no idea that there was such a close bond between the two. Do you think he was somehow taking Tony's place in the Judge's eyes?"

"That could be part of the answer. Although he has known Stephen since he was quite a young boy. He was the adopted son of a village couple who had a small-holding just outside Chilworth. To help with the family finances, the husband would often spend a day or two each week up here as handyman-cum-gardener, while his wife would help out in the house. All this, of course, was before Mother, Janet and I came to live here."

"If the family weren't too financially secure there must have been a fair amount of sacrifice to enable Stephen to be put through medic training," I said.

"Oh, that was the dear old Dad's doing," Judy smiled. "He paid for all that. He grew to be really fond of the boy. And still is."

"And Dr. Grant's foster parents?"

"The husband died some years ago, but the old lady still keeps house for Stephen. He's a devoted son."

"At one time you were engaged to him? What really soured that?"

"We must have been the most unromantic couple imaginable. Thrown together more like brother and sister . . . Friends, yes; but lovers, no."

I cast a sidelong glance in Judy's direction and couldn't help feeling that Stephen Grant had certainly missed a trick or two. Catching my eyes she slightly misinterpreted my thoughts.

"I'm not a virgin, Michael, if that's what you're thinking. It would have been rather difficult for an impressionable young girl like myself to have spent three years at art college without forming the odd romantic alliance."

I grinned. "How odd were they?"

"You know very well what I mean,"

she said with mock severity. "You're only trying to embarrass me, while all I'm endeavouring to do is to get the records straight between us. You see, you're rather an unusual man, Michael O'Hara, and I'm beginning to feel that I'm coming to rely a little too much on you. For an independent young female that could be bad news."

"For a dependent male that could be good news."

"You're not dependent on anyone or anything," she replied. "I've seldom known anyone who's so self-reliant. You're tough in many ways, and I've no doubt could be extremely rough if need be, but under it all there's a strong vein of tenderness."

"Me, tender?" I chortled. "You've got the wrong vegetable there." And I thought of several gentlemen now languishing in Her Majesty's gaols, plus a couple who were helping to promote the well-being of daisies from the root, who would have scoffed at any idea of Mrs. O'Hara's boy, Michael, having any claim to tenderness.

"Play it down, if you like," she murmured serenely. "But I know what I know. You might be something of a chauvinist in your way, but I can't imagine you ever striking a woman."

"Given sufficient provocation and I guess I could get round to it."

"Supposing I was to slap your face now — for nothing at all. What would you do? Lose your temper and hit me back?"

"Try it and see," I suggested.

Reaching forward she tapped me lightly on the cheek.

"This is where I provide the provocation," I said, and cradling her face in my hands I kissed her soundly and then one hand, almost of its own volition, slipped down to cup one full young breast.

"Hey, a girl's got to come up for air sometime," she gasped, ungluing her lips from mine but leaving my hand pleasantly in situ.

"There's some chemistry about you

that makes me feel as callow as a teenager on his first date," I said.

"Then let's try a little more chemistry," she murmured, and guided my hand beneath her gown to warm, firmly rounded flesh. As my hand brushed across her taut nipple I felt a slight shudder shake her body.

Her eyes held mine questioningly. "Are things happening too fast for you?"

"Never too fast for me," I replied. "But I've a great regard for you, Judy. A girl as attractive as you has every right to think of fulfilled relationships eventually leading to marriage. Whilst my bachelor state doesn't make that impossible, I'm afraid my present vocation could lead to early widowhood for any girl unwise enough to tie themselves to me . . ."

"I'm not asking you to marry me, Michael. Just asking you to love me. Because I need loving so badly. Think of it as therapy, if you like, but for the first time in my life I feel the need to be wanted and cared for, by you, and only you."

"Don't let me hurt you, Judy," I murmured between kisses. "I may not be as tender-hearted as you imagine."

"I'm willing to take my chance on that," she whispered. "I know you said that I make you feel like a teenager, but there's a perfectly good bed — a double-bed, as it happens — upstairs in my room. If only you could feel adult enough to share it with me."

With scant ceremony I pulled her to her feet, her dressing-gown parting nicely to reveal that the breast I had been gently fondling had its replica. "What are we waiting for? Suddenly I feel more adult that I've ever felt before."

"And is it a nice feeling, Michael?" she asked as she led the way to the stairs.

"Unless you were a man and were made aware of a certain tightening of the loins, you could have little idea of what a nice feeling it is."

"Perhaps I can guess," she smiled and ascended the stairs with commendable alacrity and a certain disarrangement of her gown that did little to allay the afore-mentioned tightness.

Once in her room, she slipped out of her night-attire and jumped into bed, pulling a single sheet up to her neck to cover her nakedness.

"Spoil-sport," I grinned. "Is that sheet really necessary?"

"For the moment — I want to lie here and watch you undress."

"Kinky!" I said, my own clothing flying off me with the speed of a fireman practising in reverse. Then noticing her eyes dwelling on the adhesive plaster that strapped the side of my rib-cage, I added, "Nothing to worry about — just a scratch. It won't, er, hinder me in anyway, I assure you."

"Some scratch," was her cryptic reply. "But tell me, Michael, will you be missed at the hotel? If you could stay the night I promise to bring you breakfast in bed."

"I won't be missed," I said, and told her about my transfer to Mrs. Martin's cottage. "But surely I rate more than just breakfast in bed?" I added.

"We'll see," she said, and reaching up for a cord-switch plunged the room into darkness.

"You're shy!"

"Perhaps, a little. But pull the curtains back."

I did as bidden and immediately the room was flooded with soft moonlight. Looking across to Judy, where her exquisite features were framed in the light-gold halo of her hair, I thought never to have seen a girl looking so wonderfully desirable before.

"It's lonely here, by myself, Michael."

Seconds later and she was lonely no more. And as I held her in my arms and experienced the wonderful, warm generosity of her love-making — a warmth that increased with mounting passion — I had a new and slightly disturbed feeling that my heart was being stolen away. A grave admission for a hard-boiled character like myself.

At last, she lay back relaxed in my arms. With eyes closed and breathing still quickened, she murmured, "Good night, my love, and thank you, thank you so much."

Gently, I eased my arm from beneath her shoulders, pulled the sheet up so that her coral-tipped breasts were covered, glanced at my watch, wondered where the time had gone, and composed myself for sleep. It had been quite a day!

It was the music of jingling crockery that awoke me the next morning. Sun was streaming into the room through the uncurtained window and Judy was just placing a tray containing coffee, milk and two cups and saucers by my bedside.

"Thought I'd join you for an early morning cuppa, before fixing our breakfast," she said.

Reaching out, I slid an arm about her waist and pulled her gently to the bed alongside me. "How do you feel, this morning?"

"Wonderful — well and truly cared for," she smiled, pressing warm lips to that part of my cheek that was still kissable above my beard. "I'm not sure that you haven't missed your true vocation, Michael."

"That of gigolo?"

"No, silly, that of therapist," and with this she began to find other parts of me that were without beard and reasonably accessible to her lips.

Well, one thing led to another and the coffee was quite cool before the pair of us surfaced again. We took a few sips and then showered together in the Judge's king-size bathroom. Once dressed and decent, we made our way downstairs where I fixed fresh coffee while Judy prepared more solid sustenance.

"I'd like to call into the hospital to see how my step-father is getting along," Judy said, once the meal was finished.

"I'll come with you, but first could we drop in at the cottage?"

"Of course, you'd better keep in with your landlady," Judy smiled. "Who knows, you may be away from the cottage on other nights."

"Are you making plans?"

"Quite definitely and shamelessly."

Later that morning, I left Judy parked outside the cottage when I called on Mrs. Martin and explained how duty had kept me away from my bed last night. She cocked a knowledgeable eye out of the window to where Judy awaited me in her Marina and said sweetly, "I trust you didn't spend too lonely a night, Michael. Now off you go. Don't keep the poor girl waiting any longer." With which she accompanied me to the door and waved to Judy.

"More of the blarney?" Judy smiled, as we moved off in the direction of Cheltenham. "All the ladies — young and old — seem to fall under your spell. Even young Mary was praising you when she and I were talking in

Andy's cottage, the other day."

"It's a burden I have to carry," I grinned. "Y'see I didn't just kiss the Blarney-stone when I was a nipper. My dad held my legs while I had a jolly good lick at it. Not that it tasted all that wonderful if memory serves me aright."

With a smile dimpling the cheek nearest to me, she reduced speed and finally halted in a small tree-fringed lay-by. "Come here, you man, you!" she said, turning in her seat and sliding an arm about me. "I'd like to sample some Blarney-Stone — even if it's second-hand."

"And the hospital?"

"Can wait for a few minutes!"

14

ARRIVING at the hospital much later than we had originally intended, one mention of the old Judge's name and we were soon directed to his private ward. Making our way along one of the interminable corridors that seem to be the official layout for so many hospitals, we were surprised to see some feverish conversation taking place between a white-coated gentleman and a couple of nurses. Noting our approach, the man headed our way. It was Dr. Stephen Grant, looking quite businesslike with a stethoscope necklace and a hypodermic syringe in one hand.

"I don't think you should go in to see your father just yet, Judy," he said.

"He's all right?"

"He is now. I'm just taking the

contents of this syringe along to be analysed."

"Don't you know what it contains?" I asked.

"No, someone masquerading as a member of the hospital staff was about to use this on the Judge. Sister, there, surprised him, shouted at the top of her not inconsiderable voice and then clouted him in the face with the clipboard she was carrying. He dropped this syringe, pushed sister to the floor and then made off."

Judy eyed the hypodermic apprehensively. "Did someone mean to harm Daddy?"

"I don't think they intended him much good," replied Dr. Grant, drily. "He certainly isn't down for any medication. Sister!" he called, "This is Judge Quinton's daughter. Please check that it's all right for him to have visitors."

"He's awake now, Doctor. Has no idea what the disturbance was all about," said the uniformed, sternly featured middle-aged woman who could well have modelled for one of the stone idols of Easter Island. "But don't stay too long, Miss Quinton."

"Thank you, sister."

"Can we hang around for the results of the analysis, Dr. Grant?" I asked.

He nodded. "It will be treated as a matter of urgency. Shouldn't take too long."

I must say that the old Judge appeared much fitter than I had expected. In fact he was in one of his more belligerent moods.

"It was young Stephen's idea to keep me here in hospital," he growled, after preliminary welcomes had been exchanged.

"But you must remain under observation now that you've had a stroke," Judy protested.

"Stroke, my foot!" retorted the old man, inelegantly. "He's just keeping me in here for my own safety, or so he says."

"Then I think it's very thoughtful of

Stephen," said Judy.

"Bah!" exploded the Judge with a mounting irascibility that must have notched his blood-pressure up to a new high. "I have work to do. Important cases are due in court."

"But only minutes ago someone tried to give you an injection. Luckily sister interrupted him," rejoined his step-daughter.

"So that's what the commotion was about," said Judge Quinton, thoughtfully.

"Certain people seem to have it in for you, one way or another," I said.

"Quite likely," he said curtly. "In my time on the bench I've sent prisoners down for a long stretch. Never did put much credence on their threats. Natural enough if you're the one who passes sentence that's going to deprive them of liberty and easy-living for a few years, then they're apt to be rather rash and fulsome with vengeful threats." He relaxed somewhat, smiled, and caught his step-daughter's hand in his own — not a customary gesture on his part, I felt certain. "I'm too long in the tooth to worry much about that sort of thing, but I don't want you to be drawn into any sort of danger, Judy."

It was at that moment that Dr. Grant entered the ward. His normally sallow cheeks looked quite ashen. "Some devil intended to kill you, sir," he said.

"What was in the syringe?" I asked.

"Strychnine — enough to see three or four men off!"

Judge Quinton's lips tightened. "Not the most comfortable way to go. That finishes it. I'm getting out of here."

"It would be most unwise," said Grant. "We'll be taking extra precautions now. Move you to another ward where intruders will have no chance of gaining access."

"I'm sure that Stephen's right," said Judy. "Please do as he says."

"Well, I'll think about it," her step-father said at last. "If it will set your mind at ease."

"A few more days' rest won't come

amiss," said Dr. Grant. "You've been over-working for years. Here's a chance to recharge your batteries."

"Just so long as certain villains don't decide to help with the recharging," replied the old Judge, drily.

"I'll give you another five minutes with your daughter, and then I'll make arrangements for your transfer," said Stephen Grant.

"To your top-security wing, I suppose," said the Judge, with unusual humour.

And so it was a little over five minutes later that Judy and I retraced our steps through hospital corridors and finally came out into fresh air that was untainted with the faint smell of ether.

"I was rather surprised to see Dr. Grant here at the hospital. I thought he was just a local G.P." I said.

"Stephen only has a small general practice. He's a specialist here at the hospital, then there's the clinic he runs for drug addicts, over Oxford way. Although the clinic is more of a philanthropy than anything else. It was first alcoholism and then drug abuse — especially among the young — that became a major interest. Although the clinic was always a bone of contention between father and him."

"I've heard that the Judge comes down hard on anyone found guilty of messing about with the unlawful supply of drugs," I said.

"True enough. Daddy does seem to have a bee in his bonnet where drugs are concerned. Stephen feels that he is helping to save young lives, but Daddy is old-fashioned, even rather bigoted about certain aspects of modern life. He's unaware of the temptations that are put in the way of youngsters, these days."

"I'm with him for part of the way on that," I admitted.

"But you're not narrow-minded, Michael."

"I'm worse than that when it comes to tackling those responsible for reaping fortunes for themselves from those who may first experiment with drugs and then find themselves addicted. The Judge may deal harshly with those convicted of drug-trafficking, but I assure you that I have dealt even more severely, in some cases you might say, terminally, with villains connected with drug crimes."

I saw Judy shiver slightly. "You really are a strange mixture of a man. Such tenderness and such violence."

"Perhaps there's a reason for some of the rough-stuff," I said, and as we drove away from the hospital I told her about my sister — without embroidery, just a simple statement of cause and effect.

"I can understand now. But will there be no end for you, Michael? Will you just carry on with this work until — well — someone proves quicker and tougher than you?"

"Never given it much thought before. But I must admit — quite recently — that I've thought of turning my talents to less demanding directions. I've even had visions of again tackling something approaching a normal nine-to-five job."

Judy took her eyes off the road for a second, coloured slightly as she saw me glancing questioningly at her, and then drove on with slightly more speed.

"What do you say to having another 'Ploughman's' for lunch today?" I asked.

"Love it! How about the *Seven Hens* just this side of Cirencester?"

"Sounds fine. Drive on, James," I grinned.

And so it was, some twenty minutes later that we found ourselves seated together under a gay umbrella in the rose-decked garden of a small but most hospitable inn, with hunks of freshly-baked bread, butter, tomatoes, lettuce, pickle and hearteningly thick slabs of farmhouse cheddar cheese on the plates before us. Judy with a modest glass of lager, and yours truly with a pint of tangy bitter to help the victuals along.

"While we're this close to Cirencester, how about calling in to see Mary at the tea-shop where she works?" Judy suggested. "I'd like to invite her and Andy over for dinner one night."

"Agreed. I've got a soft spot for that young couple."

We lingered for a while longer in the June sun, my companion still sipping at her original glass of lager, but with Mrs. O'Hara's favourite son enjoying a refilled tankard.

"If you were to leave this — the organization that you work for now — have you any idea what you'd like to do?"

Judy asked, giving me a level glance from those glorious grey-blue eyes.

"Oh, yes! Before I joined the Gnome's band of unhappy warriors I was a chartered surveyor — with letters after my name, no less! I've been wondering if it wouldn't be rather pleasant to settle here in the Cotswolds and try to drum up enough commissions to help me keep body and soul in the manner to which they have rarely been accustomed."

"I had no idea that you had any profession behind you," my companion murmured.

"Well, it's not so much behind me," I smiled, "As being well thought of for the future. But first, I must try to help INIT smash this new drug caper that's surfaced in these parts."

"If I can help you, Michael."

"Well, you're certainly involved in the whole affair, for some reason or other. Just as your sister, Janet, appears to have been, as well as your stepfather. I wonder what is in that packet or parcel that those villains were so desperately keen on getting, the other night?"

Judy shrugged. "I have no idea. Certainly, nothing like that has arrived in the post over the last few days."

"I guess we'll get to know in good time. Shall we push off to Cirencester and try to have a word or two with young Mary?"

"It will be too early for one of your Cream Teas," she laughed.

"Suppose so, but we can always have a modest cuppa. It will help to take away the taste of this bitter," I grunted, supping the last mouthful from my tankard.

We arrived at the tea-shop in that off-beat period when lunches were over and there were only a few requiring early tea. Mary acknowledged us with a smile as soon as we entered the low-beamed tea-room.

"How's Andy getting along on his first day?" I asked.

"He telephoned me during his midday break. He mentioned something that he thought you should know." Her brow creased for a moment in thought. "Ah, yes, it's about an old chap who was working at a large farmhouse recently bought by Mr. James Luckin. The old fellow's name is Spriggs — Bill Spriggs. He was doing some thatching at this farmhouse and took a nasty fall from a ladder. Andy overheard a snatch of conversation and it seems that someone purposely misplaced the ladder so that as he came down off the roof it slipped from under him."

Judy glanced at me. "Luckin — that's the man who was trying to blackmail me at the *Pig and Parsnip*."

"The same unsavoury gentleman."

"Andy also said that this same man drove up in a Rolls Royce this morning and went straight round to the rear section of the factory that's out of bounds to most of the workers," Mary added.

"Thanks. I wonder whether it would be worthwhile contacting Mr. Spriggs," I said.

"I know where he lives," remarked Judy. She smiled. "I suppose directly we've finished our tea his cottage will be the next port of call. A chauffeuse's work is never done!"

"You're a mind-reader — an absolute telepathic wonder. Try some more cold milk in that tea so that you can drink it straight down and we can be on our way," I said.

"Slave-driver," she rejoined. But I noticed that she didn't tarry over her tea. She seemed quite as keen as myself to have words with Bill Spriggs.

It didn't take us long to reach the old thatcher's minute dwelling — a typical Cotswold cottage, set at the end of a row of similar small dwellings, which Judy told me had, at one time, housed a number of local weavers. Small the cottages may have been, but from the stone-tiled roofs to the warm limestone walls they had a permanence about them that put to shame some of the rectangular brick boxes that modern developers struggle to cram into any limited spaces available on the outskirts of the main metropolitan areas.

In answer to our second knock, a plump, white-haired country-woman opened the heavily-planked front door. It took only the most elementary detective work, having taken note of the smudges of flour on bare arms and one cheek, to guess at the occupation that we had interrupted.

"Sorry I were a moment or two in answerin' door. Busy baking out back, m'dears," she said.

"Hello, Mrs. Spriggs. Please forgive this sudden call," Judy apologised, "but my friend, Mr. O'Hara, would like to have a word with your husband if that's at all possible."

"Ooh, m'dear," she said. "If it's about work I'm sore afraid that my pore Bill 'as done his back in, an' doctor reckons it 'ull be another week or so before he can move around freely again."

"It's not about work, Mrs. Spriggs," I assured her. "Just a friendly chat. Nothing to worry him."

"Well, then, I guess you might as well come through to the back. He's out there sunnin' hisself, at the moment. Wouldn't be at all su'prised effen he hasn't dozed off by now." So saying, she ushered us through the cottage until we stood on stone steps leading down to a snug little garden, completely walled-in, the lime-stone slabs enhanced by a profusion of rambling roses and fragrant honeysuckle.

"Waken thyself, Bill. Folks here to see you," said Mrs. Spriggs, pushing gently at her husband's shoulder where he sat slumped comfortably in a well-cushioned chair in the partial shade cast by a gnarled old apple-tree, already bearing a generous crop of small apples.

"Eh, whassat!" exclaimed the old chap, rubbing at his eyes and yawning prodigiously. "What be ye wanting, lass?"

"It's not me who's a-wanting, but these good folk here. You'll remember Miss Quinton, the Judge's daughter?"

"Aye, that I do. Sorry I can't get out o' this chair to greet 'ee, Miss, but me back feels as though it needs an oil-can taking to it."

"Sorry to hear about your accident, Bill," said Judy. "We called in because my friend wondered how you're getting along."

"Effen it's thatching work you've in mind, I don't reckon I'll be able to take anything on until the end o' the month. But sit yourselves down. Annie, how about some tea for these two young folk? I could do with a cup, myself."

Directly his wife was well out of earshot he cast a quizzical glance in our direction, one hoary eyebrow seeming to have a will of its own. "It weren't no accident, y'know."

"Are you sure, Bill?" Judy said.

"Missie, man an' boy I've been up and down ladders since I took up the craft o' thatching along o' my old Dad. In all that time I've come to 'ave a healthy regard for ladders — short 'uns and tall 'uns. They're mighty useful things, you understand, but not to be trifled with, an' that's a fact."

"So you think this so called accident was arranged?" I ventured.

"Mister, I don't think, I knows," he replied bluntly.

"But why would anyone want to harm you?" asked Judy.

"'Cos I poked me nose where it wasn't wanted, I reckon. The man what's bought Yelland's old farmhouse, name of Luckin, has a fair number o' furriners working for 'im. Guess he couldn't find any o' them that was any good at thatching which was why I got the job. Most of these others were working inside, ripping things out and installin' a central heating system. Well, a few days ago, with the new thatch all but completed, I took time out to have a nose inside the house. They'd certainly smartened up the old place but what I found surprisin' was the way they had extended and fixed up the cellar. It were large enough in Yelland's day but these people have well-nigh doubled its size."

"Maybe this Mr. Luckin is fond of his wine and intends to keep a good stock by him," I said.

"No sir, I'd wager it ain't nothing like that. D'you see there's a heating plant down there now that was already turned on and making the place swelterin' hot. It weren't no good for a wine-cellar."

"Were they drying out new concrete or rendering?" I suggested.

"Dunno about that. All I do know is that a big Aussie bugger — beg pardon Miss — caught me down there and marched me back into the garden in double-quick time — an' none too gently at that."

"And the accident?"

"I've got no real proof mind you, but I'm certain sure that someone fixed my ladder so that it slid out from under me when I were halfway down."

"Is your back still very painful, Bill?" Judy asked.

"Better'n it were, Miss," said Mrs. Spriggs, answering up for her husband, as she placed a large tray of tea-things and oven-hot scones on the rustic table before us. "If you ask me, he should be getting compensation for a fall like that. Tisn't as though my Bill's a young man, an' he might just as easily have broken his neck." And then with a complete change of subject she turned to Judy and me and said, "Which jam would you like with the scones? Here's home-made strawberry and damson, or I've a nice bramble-jelly back in the kitchen."

"The strawberry jam looks really nice, Mrs. Spriggs," Judy replied.

"And I'll make a beast of myself with the damson jam," I smiled.

It was well on into the afternoon before we were able to detach ourselves from the simple hospitality of these two kindly old Cotswold folk. When we were on the point of leaving, with Judy insisting on helping Mrs. Spriggs with the washing-up, that old Bill Spriggs beckoned me closer to him.

"Effen you ask me there's some strange goin's on at Yelland's old place," he said. "Besides them there cellars, there do be a great deal of comings and goings. I haven't mentioned it to the missus, o' course, but I happen to know that one o' their top fields, lying well clear of bush an' tree, has been cleared of rocks and such-like with the grass mowed real short — a wicked waste of good green grazing I thought at the time — an' this Luckin gent is planning on using it as his private airfield. An' you know what? Danged if I didn't hear a plane buzzing low over here the other night — at least that's what I thought it were . . . "

"It was a plane, all right. I heard it, and saw it, myself. Only a small craft, quite capable of making a safe landing on a large, cleared field."

"There you are then, Mister O'Hara. They're up to something up at that place," and laying a horny finger in conspiratorial gesture alongside his nose he added. "You seem more than a mite int'rested in this Luckin an' his set-up. Now I ain't asking no questions of you, mind, but I'll keep my eyes an' ears open, when I'm out and about again, and pass on anything what seems unusual-like."

"Thanks, Bill," I said, palming a crisply folded piece of legal tender into his calloused hand, before joining Judy and taking our farewell of the old couple.

15

TWO days passed with little out of the ordinary occurring, apart from consultations with Andy as to how best I could break into the health food firm for a look-see one night.

Most of those two days I spent in seeing as much of Judy as possible — and you can read into that whatever you wish! It was on the morning of the third day when I was awakened in Judy's bedroom by the sounds of someone moving around downstairs. Judy beat me to the bedroom door. Slipping on a dainty dressing-gown that was frothy with lace, she cautiously opened the door and peered out. There came the sound of an unguarded cough from downstairs.

There was a rather quizzical expression on her face as she turned to me and said, "It's father!"

"What's he doing out of hospital?" I murmured, slipping out of bed and donning clothes with all the alacrity of a guy who has an urgent errand several miles away.

"Now don't panic," she grinned. "I'll slip down and see if he's all right."

Just how all right the old Judge would be if he discovered that I had spent the night with his daughter, I was not too sure.

Several minutes later when Judy returned I was relieved to see that she was still smiling. "It's unlikely that you'll be sent down for a stretch," she said. "My step-father is satisfied that you stayed the night here only to — er — protect me."

"If he believes that load of eye-wash," I said inelegantly, "I don't think much of his judicial perceptiveness. But how is it that he's out of hospital?"

"He just up and quit. Said there's important work to be done and he's not hiding himself away to please anybody."

When Judy and I finally descended the stairs together it was to find old man Quinton tucking into a remarkably substantial breakfast that he must have got together for himself. Certainly there was nothing to suggest the invalid in the amount of nourishment he was packing away under his belt.

He must have guessed my thoughts.

"First decent meal I've had in days," he said, around a mouthful of bacon. "Some fool at the hospital decided that it would do me no harm to lose a few pounds in weight. If you ask me it was nothing short of malice on the part of that battle-axe of a ward-sister."

"Was that the same sister whose prompt action prevented someone from giving you a veinful of strychnine?" Judy asked sweetly.

"Yes, I suppose that was the woman. I've at least that to thank her for," he replied with unabashed truculence. He paused with a forkful of tomato midway to his mouth, and the crowsfeet that cornered his eyes beneath the grizzled brows creased to a rare smile. "I'd give a lot to hear what she has to say when she finds my bed empty."

"Didn't you ask permission or advise the hospital authorities that you were leaving?" his step-daughter said severely.

"Of course I didn't!" he snorted. "Should never have been kept there in the first place."

"Stephen only arranged it for your own good."

"That's as maybe, but I need to get back into circulation. There's something going on in this district that needs a team of investigators." He glanced at me. "I'm well aware of your capabilities, Michael, but you must admit that it's rather short-sighted of the powers-that-be to send only one man into the field when there's a whole gang of villains hell-bent for infamy in these parts."

"You're certain that there is a gang, sir?"

"There must be," he said, placing knife and fork fastidiously alongside each other on his empty plate. "Here we've had two murders in a matter of days, plus the fact that thugs have broken into my house and threatened me. Which reminds me, Judy, I suppose we haven't received any package through the post yet? I 'phoned my rooms yesterday and my secretary tells me that a packet arrived which, on my previous instructions she placed in the office safe. Would you believe that someone had the audacity to break into my rooms? Fortunately, they were disturbed by the caretaker and fled before they could force the safe. My secretary has now sent the package on to me by registered post."

"The contents of that package seem to have an importance in the scheme of things," I said.

"Exactly," he replied. "Frankly, it was the news from my rooms that decided me to leave hospital. Now I'm going up to Town, today, my girl. If the package arrives during my absence don't put it in the safe in my study, but hide it away in any likely or unlikely place that you can think of. Directly I return from Town we'll open it up and see just what it is that these scum place so much value on."

"Will you be driving up to London?" I asked, thinking that despite his protestations of well-being he really looked his age today — and more — with a greyness of features and slight tremor of fingers that I had not noticed before.

"No," he said, reluctantly. "I'll be taking the train. Will you drive me in to Cheltenham in about an hour's time please, Judy? I'll take a shower and spruce myself up first."

"Of course," his step-daughter assured him, and then with a sideways glance in my direction. "Perhaps Michael wouldn't mind accompanying us — he's so insistent on the necessity to protect me."

The old boy shot me a glance from those slate-blue eyes. "He can come. In fact I'm becoming used to having him around at all sorts of usual and, er, unusual hours."

"He's really not at all well," said Judy, as the Judge levered himself to his feet and climbed the stairs at a rather laboured rate. "Stephen is quite right, he needs a thorough rest. I'm certain that Janet's death hit him much harder than he allowed anyone to suspect. And other events haven't helped to settle him. I wonder if I can coax him into taking some sort of cruise holiday? A change of scene plus three or four weeks lazing around aboard ship would do him the world of good."

Later, as we drove across to Cheltenham, Judy put this to him. The old boy would have none of it.

"Don't worry about me m'girl," he said. "There's a fair amount of quite important work to be cleared up; then I'll stand down and potter around home for a while. The thought of wallowing in a deck-chair on a cruise-liner has no appeal at all."

There was no doubt that a shower, shave and change of clothes — or maybe it was that breakfast — had wrought some improvement in the Judge's appearance. He was looking more like his old self as we saw him aboard the London-bound train.

"And now what?" Judy asked. "Shall we spend some time here or have you anything else in mind?"

"So far as you're concerned I always seem to have something else in mind," I grinned, but while we're in Cheltenham I'd like to look up my boss, Sir Norman Norrick, if I can find out where he's staying."

"How will you find out?"

"A 'phone call to Inspector Marlow should produce the address — if I ask nicely!"

And so it proved. The Inspector raised no objections about divulging the Gnome's pied-a-terre. I mentioned Judge Quinton's flit from hospital, but he already knew about the old man's cavalier leave-taking.

A 'phone call established the fact that the Gnome wasn't expected to be home until around two o'clock that afternoon, so after some light shopping, we lunched at a splendid little hotel, with sloping lawns amid sylvan splendour, just off one of the spacious tree-lined avenues, which together with Regency terraces and colourful parks makes this town such an attractive place. Henry Skillicorne, the sea-captain who enclosed the well of alkaline spring-water, arranged for the assembly room and spa, and was also responsible for much of the tree-planting in the town is deservedly remembered by a fulsome epitaph in the parish church. There is a spacious graciousness about parts of Cheltenham that takes one easily back through the years to more leisurely days. As we walked the wide streets and passed through the fashionable shopping centre I occasionally paused to check the prices of desirable properties, as advertised in various estate-agents' windows.

"Are you really serious about a change of occupation?" Judy asked, as I paused yet again to scan coloured photographs in an agents' window.

"Absolutely! I'm not without the odd bob or two tucked away. I can either set up in my own business or buy in to a partnership."

"Won't you find life too boring then?" she asked.

"Not it, Judy. I really like houses, from humble cottages to grand mansions," I paused. "Would you find it boring to be tied down to someone who really cares for you?"

She eyed me quizzically. "Would this be some sort of proposal, Michael, m'boyo?"

"Yes, I want to make an honest woman of you."

"And not before time, I'd say. But is this a proposal of marriage or convenience?"

"These last few days I've been thinking it carefully through, my love,"

I said firmly. "I want to marry you."

With which I surprised myself and startled a few passers-by by drawing Judy into a receptive position and kissing her soundly.

"Michael, you're behaving just like a love-lorn teenager," she chided, with a smile.

"I'm aware of it. Isn't it nice? Wasn't it George Bernard Shaw who said something about Youth being wasted on the Young?"

"He has something there," she said, gently ruffling my beard with a slim forefinger. "But are you sure you're in the right mood to see Sir Norman?"

"He'll have to take me, no matter what mood I'm in."

"So there," she laughed.

Minutes later, we were standing before the portals of a straggling, single-storied habitation whose foundations must have covered nearly an acre of ground.

"Phew! Your boss does himself well. Do you want me along, Michael? I can easily wait for you?" Judy said.

"Yes, on both counts, Judy."

"Won't Sir Norman think it strange that you've brought me along with you?"

"The Gnome will think it strange enough that I've sought him out here in Cheltenham. A little extra surprise won't be noticed — especially after I've tendered my resignation. The wee fellow's language is likely to be most picturesque, but take no notice. I'm certain he can't spell half the words he uses."

"So you're actually going to tell him now, that you'll be finished with his organization once this present investigation has been dealt with?"

"S'right!"

My companion eyed me speculatively. "I've a feeling that you're using me, Michael."

"Me — using you?"

"Yes, to help cushion Sir Norman's wrath."

"Nothing was further from my mind.

Who knows, the old boy may probably be only too pleased to be shot of me. Shall we see if the great man is available?"

The suave gentleman who answered the door could have stepped straight out of a Wodehouse novel. If we would care to wait in the hall he would see if we could intrude on his master, although we were without an appointment. And this last a breach of etiquette that was not to be encouraged.

"Golly, a butler, no less," whispered Judy watching the dark-suited retainer glide off down a passage-way.

"There are still a few of them about, although these days they have to be carefully vetted."

"Why?"

"Too many of 'em finance an early retirement by selling their memoirs to one of the Sunday newspapers. These days valets, nannies, even parlour-maids, as well as butlers can make a nice thing out of biographical facts — probably larded with a soupcon of fiction. I'm telling you, my girl, we'll not give any servants house-room when we set up together."

"Because of the wild parties we'll be throwing?"

"No. Because of the obvious vocal enjoyment with which you finally surrender yourself to my love-making. Although I suppose we could sound-proof our bedroom."

"Michael!" she exclaimed, sudden colour flooding to her cheeks, but perforce lapsed into silence as the faithful retainer once more sloped into view.

"If you will kindly follow me. Sir Norman will see you in the library," he said in his beautiful plummy accent.

Obediently, we followed him down the passageway, with a carpet-pile underfoot thick enough to have muffled the sound of an advancing squad of infantry. There were similar signs of opulence in pictures and porcelain as we progressed. Strangely enough I had never thought of the Gnome being in the money with such a capital 'M'.

Pausing at a beautifully polished mahogany door, the butler knocked obsequiously and in answer to a command from within silently ushered us into a room that housed at least a couple of thousand books. Not paperbacks, these, but fine leather-bound volumes. Books that lined the walls from floor to ceiling and were in random piles on chairs and tables. The Gnome was working at a magnificent desk that must have been worth a small fortune in its own right, and so placed that anyone seated at it commanded a view of an immaculately-kept garden.

"And to what do I owe this visit?" he asked rather acidly, once the butler had smoothly withdrawn his presence.

"After we've finished with this Cotswold caper I shall be handing in my resignation. Thought it best for me to tell you personally than resort to a letter."

For a few seconds the Gnome's normally rubicund complexion deepened to a fetching shade of mauve. "You want to do *what*?" he finally exploded.

"Retire from INIT."

"Why?" And this last with all the venom of a poisoned dart leaving a blowpipe.

"I've other plans."

"Such as?"

"Miss Quinton has agreed to marry me. I don't want to lead her into too early a widowhood."

"But you've been with us for quite a time now, m'boy — and you're still hale and hearty, aren't you?"

"Only just — thanks to my own efforts."

"Oh Michael, you know that if the going gets too ruddy rough we always send back-up personnel to help out."

"Never noticed it in the past," I said bleakly.

"Look here, m'boy," said the Gnome in a surprisingly conciliatory tone, "and let me include you in this, Miss Quinton, since I'm sure that Mr. O'Hara has more or less told you of the type of investigation he is engaged in."

"Rather more than less," I put in.

"Of course, quite natural in the circumstance," my diminutive boss carried on smoothly. "But it is imperative that you stay with this case for a while longer."

"I've already said that I intend to see this one through."

"Good! Good! And with luck I believe we may be on the point of wrapping this one up. Duclos 'phoned from Paris yesterday to tell me that Laura Banks skipped out of France a few days ago."

"Bordello Lil back in the drug trade?" I said, giving Laura Banks the name by which she was known to most of the Interpol fuzz. "Do you think she fits into this connection?"

"You must remember how thick she was with Jimmy Luckin until things became too warm for her over here, with suspected drug-trafficking and the odd spot of white-slaving marked down to her. She skipped across to the Continent, Marseilles, we believe, although neither Duclos nor Interpol were able to lay a finger on her. Now we suspect that she and a companion boarded a light aircraft the other night and accomplished, literally, a moonlight flit, heading in this direction!"

"Do we know who her companion was?" Despite my recent plea for retirement I found myself strangely interested in the comings and goings of any villains likely to be associated with illegal drugs.

The Gnome paused for a moment and turned his beady-bright eyes in Judy's direction. "So far as we can ascertain, it was Miss Quinton's stepbrother who accompanied her."

Judy paled. "I know nothing of this. Nor does my step-father, I'm sure."

"Of course, Miss Quinton. Your step-brother may be, shall we say, something of a black sheep, but we are quite sure that neither the Judge nor yourself are at all implicated in any connection with drug-trafficking."

"Are you sure that it was Tony Quinton and Bordello Lil who flew in from the Continent?" I asked.

"Duclos seemed quite certain. As you may know, Tony Quinton was, or is, a remarkably clever chemist. We now believe that he may be responsible for manufacturing this Mega-H crap — er, pardon, Miss Quinton — in the first place. Last week, acting on information from one of his undercover boys, Duclos arranged for a certain laboratory on the northern outskirts of Paris to be raided. He was too late. The birds had flown. All they discovered was the aforementioned undercover gent with his throat cut."

16

JUDY shuddered. "These people seem to kill without a second thought."

"You must remember how much money is tied up in any connection with illegal drugs," the Gnome said. "Fortunes are being made from other folks' misery and degradation. These villains kill all right, not only by direct murder but by bringing thousands upon thousands to the living-death of drug-dependency. And this Mega-H seems to be the most vicious muck that has been pushed, so far."

"Then if Michael stays to help bring this gang to justice, I want to join your — your active list."

The Gnome pursed his little rosebud mouth. "I'm not sure that I can agree to that, m'dear. I've a notion that from now on matters may start getting really rough. They usually do when we step too close on the heels of these characters. Frankly, O'Hara might find you more of a hindrance than a help. I must be blunt about this. Obviously he cares for you, and it's quite possible that if these people suspect that he can be influenced by threatening your safety they'll readily seize the chance."

"I must say that I agree with you," I put in. "It would be far better for you to disappear for the time being, Judy. Aren't there friends or relatives you can visit in some other part of the country?"

"An excellent suggestion," said Sir Norman.

"I'm sorry, Sir Norman, but I insist on staying here with Michael. I may not be of overmuch help but I'll certainly endeavour not to get in his way."

The Gnome tut-tutted gently and then looked at me with an unspoken question. I shrugged resignedly. I knew Judy well enough by now to know that if she had made up her mind on a certain course of action there wasn't much that I or anyone else could do to change her mind.

"When you two marry I can see who'll be wearing the trousers," remarked the Gnome with some asperity.

Judy looked at me and laughed. "Sir Norman's trying to turn you off me."

"Anything but that," the little man said. "From what I know of some of Mr. O'Hara's past liaisons, I think he's finally made a wise choice."

"Would you care to go into further detail about these — er — liaisons?"

The Gnome's beady little eyes twinkled wickedly. "Perhaps, some other time," and then, turning to me. "Anything new to report?"

I quickly filled him in on the gleanings of the past couple of days, mentioning my suspicions of the health food firm and old Bill Spriggs' information about Jimmy Luckin's new place.

"I'm sure that the turd, beg pardon, Miss Quinton, that villain, Luckin, is up to his eyebrows in this caper. The news that his former girl-friend, Laura Banks, has rejoined him makes that almost a certainty."

"Would he have brains to mastermind a large-scale drug exploit like we reckon this to be?" I queried.

"Not bloody likely," said the Gnome, "but his underworld set-up would be mighty handy to anyone wanting to peddle drugs on a wide scale. No, Luckin's not Mister Big in this Cotswold connection. It would need someone with far more grey matter between the ears to organize this lot."

"I'm planning on giving both the health food firm and Luckin's place a look-over," I said.

"Very necessary, but quietly Michael. Don't stick your neck out so far that the chopper falls on it."

"I'll take care," I assured him. "By the way, have the analysts come up with any findings regarding the breakdown of this Mega-H drug?"

He shook his head. "All they know

for sure is that its use induces a greatly heightened euphoria plus having a strong aphrodisiac effect. It's heroin-based all right, but the additive not only eliminates any soporific tendencies but quickly raises dependency to the screaming level."

"Surely the backroom boys must be able to find out what this additive is?"

"They'll find out in time," he agreed, pulling thoughtfully at the lobe of one ear. "At the moment all they will say is that it's of botanical origin."

"Just like heroin and cocaine?"

"Exactly. But remember, m'boy, that there are hundreds, perhaps thousands of drugs and medicines that have been obtained from plants over the years. And most efficacious many of them have been, and still are of course, ask any modern herbalist. Who knows, there may still be plants around the world, especially in the more inaccessible parts, that have their medicinal secrets to impart. But right now, or at this moment in time, as our politicians would say, whilst we know only too well how potent this new substance is we don't bloody well know whether it comes from leaf or root, from berry or seed, and we're certainly without any idea what the parent plant can be. I understand that the next move has been to approach experts from Kew and similar establishments."

"Most of our modern drug sources — certainly those that are abused so often, cocaine, heroin, marijuana — are grown in the tropical or sub-tropical parts of the world," I said thoughtfully.

"True enough," the Gnome agreed, "although we must remember that Indian hemp can be grown in many countries of more temperate conditions. The secretion of narcotic resin may be less abundant in plants grown in cooler climates but we have still found hemp being grown out-of-doors here in Britain."

"A point that has occurred to me,"

I put in, "is the fact that not only is Tony Quinton on record as being an accomplished chemist, but I understand that soon after his release from prison he spent some time out East."

"Ye-es, I know all about that," murmured the Gnome, thoughtfully, "but don't start putting two-and-two together and make them come to five, m'boy. Young Quinton's ability and areas of travel may just be coincidence. Remember we have no idea what plant provides their additive, nor where it grows. It could equally be some moss or lichen native to the Tundra or Arctic regions as some exotic growth demanding the heat of the tropics."

"When I pay a visit to the health food firm and Jimmy Luckin's new abode I may come up with something worthwhile."

"It's possible," agreed the Gnome, "but as I've said, do take every precaution. I don't like dragging the police in on some of our nefarious ventures — at the very least your visits will count as breaking and entering — but should anything go wrong, feel free to contact Inspector Marlow at any time. He'll give you all the backing that he can."

"I'll only embroil the fuzz in things get really hairy."

"I'm sure of it, m'boy. And make sure that this young lady doesn't run into any kind of trouble that you can't handle for her."

I glanced at Judy and smiled. "How about telling her to look out for me?"

"Now that is a thought," he said. "Before you go, Miss Quinton, you may find this of some future use." And reaching into the top-right-hand drawer of his desk he produced a useful looking Beretta, together with a folded, typed document. "Sign this, m'dear, just to keep things reasonably legal." And then as he saw Judy's hesitation, he added, "have no qualms about accepting and using this automatic if events demand it. The people you are going up against are outright villains. To protect themselves they will kill — in fact I'm sure they have already done so — in the course of their bloody trade. So sign, just here!"

With a quick movement Judy scribbled her signature on the document and then as swiftly slid the automatic into her handbag.

"Ammunition?" I queried.

"It's already loaded, but here's some spare," he said, diving his hand back into the drawer and pushing a couple of small oiled-paper wrapped packets in my direction. "Well, good huntin'," he said, dismissing us. "And look out for her, Michael, we don't want you to become a widower before she becomes a widow, do we?"

His amused cackle at his own joke was the last we heard as we left him in that beautiful book-lined room.

Minutes later, as Judy and I were leaving the house, I paused halfway down the front drive to look back at the Gnome's Cheltenham pad.

"Envious?" Judy asked, mistaking my speculative look.

"Hell, no. Too many windows to clean," I grinned. "I was really trying to assess its market value. I should think it would need an oil-rich sheik with sackfuls of loot to be counted as a prospective buyer. Y'know, my little boss must be worth his weight in gold. There's something near a quarter-of-a-million pounds freehold there, without valuing the ritzy contents. I had no idea the Gnome was so well-heeled. He must look on his work with INIT as a hobby."

"I believe you really are envious, Michael."

"Not a bit of it. It's just raised the odd question mark, though. I doubt whether his job as head of our British section, would provide the Gnome with enough money to pay for the lighting and heating of that place."

"Don't worry yourself, Michael. I know that with your lowly position with Sir Norman's team you'll only be able to afford a two-up and two-down cottage, when you make an honest woman of me."

"With usual offices, of course."

"Naturally, and preferably with an inside loo, rather than one that needs a route-march to the bottom of the garden."

"Very romantic on a moonlit night," I offered.

"There's a time and place for romance," she replied.

"I'll just have to see what I can manage," I smiled.

It was later that afternoon when I had more serious words with Judy.

"I'll do the health food firm first. I'll go in just before dusk. It will be light enough to look around but not so dark that I'll need to flash a torch."

"You're not going alone," she replied.

"It will be best. With only one of us around there'll be less kerfuffle should things go wrong. If I have to make a hasty exit there'll be only myself to think about."

"I'm sorry, Michael, you're *not* going alone."

It was an argument that I only partially won. Eventually she was by my side as I drove up to the outskirts of Bibury that evening. For the purpose of this exercise we had changed over from the Marina to my MG, which could power its way around these Cotswold lanes at a very fair turn of speed. Now, as we approached the low buildings of the health food firm I cut the engine and coasted quietly down a gentle slope to finally stop in a tree-lined part of the road. "I still wish I was making this trip alone," I said, leaning across to kiss Judy before easing myself out of the driving-seat.

"You've argued me out of going inside with you, Michael, but I insist on at least waiting out here, ready for a speedy departure, if needed," she said, one strong young arm encircling my neck to pull me down for another loving salutation. "I'll slip into the driving-seat and have the passenger door unlocked for you. All you'll have to do will be to jump in and we'll be away."

Earlier, I had been able to contact Andy during the course of his deliveries. Thanks to his detailed directions I had a clear layout of the place in mind. Also, thanks to Andy, I had no fear of a strident alarm bell alerting the neighbourhood. One of his last chores had been to render the burglar alarm voiceless. It's amazing how even the most sophisticated alarm-system can be silenced by judiciously snipping a couple of wires!

Andy, good lad, had also wanted to accompany me but I had impressed upon him his need to establish an unbreakable alibi so that there was no chance of him being connected with my visit. He was far too valuable in his present position, with the ability to glean inside information if the firm were not on the up-and-up.

Now, after a quick and none too elegant a scramble over an eight-foot high stone wall, I soft-shoed it towards the rear of the building, quietly slipped the catch on a rear window that had been 'doctored' by Andy, and found myself in the firm's packing department. There were shelves and storage bays carrying a varied assortment of cartons and boxes, and down the centre of the room were three large zinc-covered work tables, bearing knives, scissors, balls of twine, coils of adhesive tape and packets of labels printed with the name and address of the firm.

On the face of it there appeared to be nothing of real interest for me here, so I tackled an inner-door, using a piece of thin plastic to slip the lock. Andy's directions had been spot-on. I found myself in an extremely well-equipped and business-like laboratory. The place was not particularly large. Judging by the combined sinks and work-benches not more than five people could be working here. Barred windows gave out on to a paved central quadrangle on one side, the opposite wall of the room bore a full complement of shelves above waist-high cupboards, stretching the full length of the room. The shelves were filled with large plastic containers, bearing labels of their contents. It amused me to see the array of vitamins and food supplements that civilization insists we need for rosy-cheeked health and zest for living. With this lot so close to hand the workers in this establishment had every chance of being among the healthiest and most virile in this neck of the woods.

However, none of the pills, powders and potions that I found either on the shelves or in the cupboards that I opened, inspected and then meticulously reclosed, were of a suspicious nature. I looked around the laboratory again. Over in a far corner was another door secured by a double-lock. It was a good lock, as well. It took several minutes of patient work with the small set of 'picks' I was carrying before I had that door opened.

At first I had thought it would reveal an ordinary cupboard or store, but instead I found myself in a claustrophobic windowless room, probably some 10-metres square, with work benches gracing three of its sides. Equipped as a small but highly-sophisticated laboratory, I guessed it was in use for much more profitable products than the larger place outside. I sniffed at some white powder heaped in a porcelain crucible, then with moistened forefinger I transferred a few grains to the tip of my tongue. It was heroin, all right, and as far as my layman's experience could judge, a pure grade of the stuff that appeared to me to be uncut by any additives.

On another bench I found a plastic container that held a quantity of greyish powder, rather more granular in form than that contained in the crucible. I gave this the same taste and smell test but was vouchsafed no clues as to its nature or origins. Checking on other equipment about the room convinced me that I had uncovered a source of illicit drug manufacture, but whether Mega-H was produced here I was unable to decide. Some say that ignorance is bliss but right then I wished my knowledge of chemistry was not so appallingly poor.

Having carefully taken samples of these two powders in a couple of minute plastic bottles, of which there were hundreds in the place, and having made sure that I had left no visible traces of my break-in, I was on the point of leaving this inner laboratory when sight of a large trunk under one of the benches caught my eye. It was locked, but not so securely that my little bunch of locksmith's friends couldn't fiddle it open. With the lid opened I found the contents were housed in a large white, opaque plastic sack. Something about the contours of the bag made me unseal the mouth of it very gingerly. My first glimpse as it fell open revealed the sight of Dr. Stephen Grant's head, with a neat bullet-hole in the centre of the brow, just above the eyes. I opened the sack further. His body was fully clothed and as his head fell forward I saw the cavernous exit where the bullet had devastated the rear of his skull. Death may have been instantaneous for the Doctor but at the moment it was far from pretty. With bile burning the back of my throat I resettled the body, closed the plastic sack and locked the lid of the trunk.

I wanted out from that place — and sharpish!

It took me a few minutes to secure the door, return to the main laboratory and from there back to the store-cum-packing department. By now dusk had really settled and I was displeased, to say the least, by the sight of twin headlights forging down the drive towards the building.

The vehicle, a Volvo estate as near as I could judge in that half-light, swung to a halt in front of the main entrance and four shadowy figures alighted. Two of them, one of whom I thought to recognise as the bulky Australian bullyboy, Eddie Moxon, came straight on for the building, the remaining couple, one of whom I could now see was struggling ineffectually in the grip of a much taller person remained by the car.

I nipped hastily across to the storeroom window that I had left conveniently opened against just such need for a speedy exit. I heard the main doors opening and was about to launch myself over the window-sill when a voice stopped me."

"We know you're here, O'Hara. We've got Judy Quinton outside. If you don't want something really unpleasant to happen to her, sport, just come here to us — with your hands pointing to the bleedin' ceiling!"

17

"YOU'VE been watching too many TV westerns," I said, trying to keep the conversation light as I came out of the store-room and found myself in a well-lit vestibule. But I kept my hands raised when I saw the muzzles of two Smith & Wessons pointing at me like twin unblinking eyes of death. Eddie Moxon, and the punkish creep who sided him, looked quite capable of triggering me into swift oblivion, should I dare but breathe too heavily for their liking.

"Frisk 'im, Charlie. But take care. He's a right smooth, quick-thinkin' bastard," said Eddie Moxon, flatteringly.

"Charlie, eh! Now that's a nice name your parents gave you. What did they do to deserve a toe-rag like you for their offspring?" I asked, as he ran his hands none too gently over my chassis.

By way of reply I received a round-arm swing, the side of the S & W connecting with the side of my head, just above the right ear, with sufficient force to cause the dusk to brighten to a multi-coloured sunset as I was felled to my knees.

"Good on you, Charlie-boy," chortled the big Australian. "That's just a friggin' love-tap compared to what I've got lined up for him." With which he used the toe of a large and heavy brogue to encourage me to my feet again.

"Shall I take a look see around, Eddie? There's that trunk. D'ya figure he coulda seen it?" asked his shifty-eyed side-kick.

"Naw! It don't matter now what he bloody saw. We'll get both him an' the girl straight back to the Boss's place. It's a friggin' good job that the Man insists on some of us casing the joint every coupla hours or so. Then there was that special errand we had . . ."

So that was it, I thought. I had been

stupid not to realise that some sort of watch might be kept on this place — especially in view of the secrets of that inner laboratory.

"You're coming out with us now, sport," said Moxon. "Don't try anything on. We've got the girl out there by our vehicle. You'd only make it hard on her."

When I finally saw Judy I mentally castigated myself for my supreme carelessness. The sight of her anguished eyes in the pale oval of her face did little for my self-esteem.

"I'm sorry, Michael, I should have kept a better look-out," she began, and then winced to sudden silence, as the tall Latin-type who held her, twisted his fingers cruelly in her hair and forced her into the front passenger seat of the Volvo estate.

"Like I said, don't get any smart ideas, bucko!" Eddie Moxon warned me as he noted the tenseness with which I watched Judy being manhandled into the vehicle. "I'd just as soon give you yours right here and now. But I happen to know that the Man would dearly like to ask you a few questions."

"The Man. Do I know him?" I asked conversationally, and was rewarded by a thump in the kidneys that helped me find a rear seat in the estate-car.

"Any need to put blinkers on 'em so they won't know where they're being took?" asked punkish Charlie.

"Why bother ourselves? It's not the sorta information they're ever gonna be able to use," said Moxon, most disagreeably. "Just get us back to the Boss as quick as you can, Marco," he added, addressing the Latin-looking character who had slid into the driving-seat.

And so we drove off. Judy in the front passenger seat beside friend, Marco, with Charlie, Moxon and myself squeezed up in matey fashion on the rear bench seat. To add to the comfort of our journey, the big Australian ape jammed the muzzle of his Smith & Wesson hard into my ribs, while Charlie — damn his eyes! — taking a cue from Marco, wrapped his dirty fingers in Judy's blonde hair to encourage her to remain fast in the seat in front of him.

Less than twenty minutes later, we swung off a narrow lane into a hedge-fringed drive that led us to the front of a straggling, double-storey, thatched farmhouse building. I had time to notice several large, barn-like outhouses, with piles of timber, quarried limestone, sand, ballast, cement and a cement-mixer, all pointing to the fact that fairly extensive construction work was still under way, before being rudely coaxed round to the rear of the farmhouse where a heavy door thudded open to a thrust of Moxon's brogue-shod foot.

"What's this, the tradesmen's entrance?" I asked as we found ourselves in a wide stone-flagged passage.

"Shut your friggin' gob or I'll fill it for you," was Eddie's impolite admonishment. Then, turning to the runt, Charlie, he added, "I reckon they're down there. Go tell the Man about our visitors — an' where does he want 'em?" With which he indicated an open door at the head of a flight of stone steps leading down to what was probably the old farmhouse cellar.

"You're to bring 'em down here, Eddie," said Charlie, a moment later, reappearing at the top of the stairs like some moronic jack-in-the-box. "I fink the Boss-man is real pleased with us."

"Right, then down you go, cocko," said Moxon, giving me such a hefty push with a ham of a hand that I was sent skittering down the flight of stone steps to finally come to rest on all fours in a most undignified manner.

The first thing that struck me was how damned hot it was down there, an enervating, humid heat which, for the first couple of breaths, the old lungs were none too happy with. The next, as I scrambled to my feet, was sight of the small reception committee of three who awaited me. Jimmy Luckin I recognised immediately, and the girl, Laura Banks, standing beside him — although she was no longer the hard-faced brassy blonde that I'd had pointed out to me months ago in one of the back purlieus of Soho, but was now well into a brunette phase with a dress cut so low in the front that I could almost see the fluff in her navel. The third member of the trio I had never seen before; a tall, stoop-shouldered man of indeterminate age, whose scarred face and thin-lipped mouth bore mute testimony to some surgeon's knife. And if these were the best features that surgery had been able to achieve, either it had been a very duff surgeon or the original looks had been nothing to write home about. At the moment he had the sort of face that only a mother could love — providing her eye-sight was not too good.

By now the others had joined me in the cellar, and having first lined us up against a wall, with a few pithy words Eddie Moxon told how he had surprised us at the health food firm.

"Did he search the small laboratory?" scar-face asked.

"Sorry, Boss, had no time to check. As you know, on this trip we were all set to pick up that trunk, but sight of these two rather threw us. Thought it best to bring 'em straight back to you."

"You did well," the Boss-man assured him, and reaching under the immaculate grey suit that he wore he produced a snub-nosed automatic whose blue-steel barrel pointed unwaveringly in my direction. "Leave these two down here — secure their hands with that first." He indicated a hank of cord lying on a nearby work-bench. "Then the three of you can get back to Bibury and fetch that trunk. We'll have to make the concrete floor of that new barn just that much deeper to accommodate dear departed Dr. Grant."

"Stephen Grant. What have you done to him?" Judy gasped.

"I'm afraid he's dead, quite dead,

step-sister dear," scar-face informed her. "Not really intended at the time, although it may well have had to come to just that, eventually."

"Step-sister! Then you must be Tony Quinton?" I said, and winced as Moxon coiled rope around my wrists as though he was using it to try to amputate my hands.

"How very perceptive of you," he sneered, paper-thin scar-tissue wrinkling at the corners of his mouth. "Sir Norman Norrick would be so pleased to know how astute you can be — at times!"

"You know Sir Norman?"

"Probably much more about him than either you or he is aware of."

"Why did you have to kill Stephen?" Judy asked. "Were you afraid that he might be able to help some of the addicts who might otherwise have become such good customers for you?"

"I doubt whether he would have been able to effect cures for any of those into our particular brand of heroin.

In any case, any cures in this part of the country would be just a tear-drop in the ocean," he gloated, gold-capped teeth gleaming in a mirthful rictus of that travesty of a face. "No, step-sister dear, the trouble was caused by him questioning some of the patients at that clinic of his. We had a slight leak of some of our wares. One of the van-drivers trying to earn on the side. Somehow, dear Stephen gleaned some information that brought him nosing too close to home for our comfort. A couple of nights ago he attempted to break into our place over Bibury way. Marco, here — a good man, a member of the Camorra, the Neopolitan version of the Mafia — took a lucky snapshot and wrote finis to the dear Doctor."

"You've absolutely no remorse about his murder, have you?" Judy said, bleakly. "But I've heard that you were always jealous of Daddy's interest in him — in the early days when you were both boys together."

"I hated Stephen Grant — and so

did my mother," Tony Quinton spat out. "But then Father dear had his reasons for encouraging Stephen into our home."

The conversation was becoming interesting but was interrupted by the deep-throated barking of a dog. Barking that gave way first to a deep growling as though the creature was worrying at something, and then followed by a high squeal of pain that rapidly diminished in sound as though the animal was leaving the immediate vicinity with a fair turn of speed.

"Moxon, see to it," Jimmy Luckin ordered. "Someone's out there. Most of the boys have been given permission to hit the highlights of Gloucester this evening. The dog must have flushed someone out."

Moving with surprising speed and silence for his bulk, the Australian ascended the stone steps in three leaping strides. Seconds later there came the sound of a scuffle up top and he reappeared dragging an unconscious body with him. It was Andy, whom he dumped none too gently at our feet.

"Found this bleedin' half-caste up there. Prob'bly the same guy that Charlie reckons on having seen pow-wowing from time to time with O'Hara. Christ knows what he did to the bleedin' dog. There ain't no sign of it now."

"Was he armed?" Luckin asked.

"Yes, with a friggin' air-pistol of all things," Moxon scoffed. "He soon dropped that when I clouted him."

"It's beginning to look as though the foundations for that new barn will have to be much deeper than we at first thought. And now, step-sister dear," Tony Quinton said, turning to Judy. "It's important that I know the exact whereabouts of a certain package that dear little Janet stole from me. It was because of this theft that I had to order her to be — er — questioned by young Gary Warren. But the fool played it all wrong. He had her on bended knees praying to him for another fix of the new drug we've produced. She admitted that she had posted the package to my dear Father's London rooms. Then, Gary, always a trifle hot-headed I'm afraid, lost his temper and strangled her instead of giving her the scare that he had originally intended to induce her to talk."

"And you had Warren killed in turn, because he'd bungled things?" I suggested.

Quinton and Luckin exchanged glances. "Actually, no. He was reprimanded, of course. Especially when we found where he had left Janet's body in the foolish notion that suicide would be suspected. But believe me, my dear fellow, we've absolutely no idea who gunned him down. All we can think is that some poacher or footpad took a dislike to his presence and blasted him with their shotgun."

At that moment, Andy stirred, raised his head and looked about him.

"Sorry, Guv," he mumbled, catching sight of me. "I know you told me I'd not be needed this evening. But, man, I just couldn't stay away. Might even have been useful to you if that bloody Doberman hadn't taken a dislike to me."

"What happened to the dog, dear boy?" Quinton asked.

Andy hunched one shoulder around so that I could see where the sleeve was ripped and the flesh of his left upper-arm badly lacerated. "I like dogs and I'm not exactly proud of what I did. But it was either the Doberman or me, so I poked the barrel of my air-gun into his ear and pulled the trigger."

"The RSPCA wouldn't approve, dear boy."

"Mebbe not, but the damned thing was working its way round to my throat, and I wouldn't have approved of that," was Andy's caustic reply.

"Tch! tch! The young are so violent these days," murmured Quinton. "But then you, dear boy, are obviously of mixed blood. No doubt your father, if he was the parent responsible for your — er — permanent suntan, bequeathed you the ability to deal effectively with attacking animals — inside and outside the jungle."

The little runt, Charlie, who had remained fairly inactive up to now, crossed the room and kicked Andy viciously in the belly.

"I liked that dog. Before we're through with you I'll tear off both your bleedin' lug-'oles!"

"All in good time," Quinton said soothingly. "Right now I want to know whether any other members of INIT or the police have any true idea of our set-up here at the farm or over at Bibury. It's also most imperative that I know just where we can lay our hands on that package that Janet stole from us. How about it, O'Hara, do you feel like answering any of those questions?"

"When Hell freezes!" I replied inelegantly.

"Oh, but I think you *can* be persuaded to tell me everything I want to know," he sneered. "Moxon, tie my dear step-sister to this bench," and he indicated a large, pine-topped work-surface. "I suggest one coil of rope around her throat to inhibit any struggling, and another round her waist, then secure her ankles."

Effortlessly, the big Australian picked Judy up and roped her to the bench.

"It's very warm down here in the growing-room," Quinton continued. "Strip her — to the waist to start with."

Obediently, grinning with lascivious pleasure, Moxon fastened a huge paw in the neck of Judy's blouse and ripped it from her, the lacy brassiere beneath being despatched with the same scant ceremony.

"You said something about this being a growing-room," I put in anxiously trying to play for time. "It's hot and humid enough for a rain forest. What do you hope to grow?"

"How perceptive of you again, dear boy. The plants that we will soon have flourishing down here are normally native to an almost inaccessible region of tropical rain forest," he said. "But there, that's of no importance to you at the moment. What should concern you is that my dear step-sister will suffer some pain — possibly embarrassment — unless you tell me what I want to know."

"Don't Michael, no matter what!" Judy called. "He intends to kill us in the end."

"Quite so, my dear, but before then I'm almost sure that I can persuade Mr. O'Hara to talk to me. There are certain niceties of torture, learnt out East, that I've unfortunately no time to demonstrate at the moment. But I have a few simple ideas, crude though they may be, that should help to loosen O'Hara's tongue. They'll certainly loosen yours, my dear."

He turned to Jimmy Luckin. "Would you care to light one of those expensive cigars that you favour?"

Obligingly, Luckin made a great

show of holding a gold lighter to the end of a six-inch barrel of tobacco of the kind that only the very rich can afford to insult their lungs with.

"And now what, Tony?" he asked.

"I want you to try stubbing it out on my dear step-sister. On her breast would be as good a place as any — for a beginning!"

"All right! All right! I'll talk," I said.

But I was too late to spare Judy. Without pausing for a second, a sadistic gleam in his dark eyes, Luckin applied the glowing end of the cigar to the curve of Judy's left breast. She could not suppress a moan of pain, and as far as her bonds would permit, her body arched convulsively.

"I'll kill you, Luckin, you bastard!" I swore.

"Opportunity would be a fine thing," Tony Quinton mocked. "Get that cigar well alight again, Jimmy, and this time try the nipple. If that doesn't loosen O'Hara's tongue, there are other places . . ."

"I've already said that I'll tell you anything you want to know," I put in sharply.

"So you have, dear boy. However, keep the cigar well alight, Jimmy. Just in case! Now, O'Hara, tell me how suspect is our presence here at the farmhouse and at the health food firm?"

"I've had my suspicions for some time," I said slowly.

"I don't want to know about *your* suspicions, dear boy. I have to know whether we have to be ready to counter anything like a police raid in the near future."

"So far as I know, the police have no evidence to warrant such an action . . . " I began, and then paused as I thought to hear the sound of soft footsteps on the stone stairway. Before I could continue, to my utter amazement Judge Quinton suddenly appeared at the foot of the steps, and held rock-steady in his hands was a lethal looking sawn-off shotgun.

"Why, hallo there, Father dear," said

his son, as nonchalantly as though his parent's visit, armed with such a murderous weapon, was an everyday occurrence.

"How I ever came to father such an amoral monster as you, I'll never know," said the old Judge, ice-blue eyes taking quick stock of the scene.

"I should think in the usual old-fashioned way," his son suggested.

"In those early days of marriage I had no idea that there was a history of mental trouble in your mother's family," the Judge continued. "Had I known I'm certain that you, Tony, would never have been born. Unfortunately, it appears that you are far from mentally stable, yourself."

"You're exaggerating," countered his son, swiftly. "I know mother was, shall we say, a little eccentric at times. But she was my mother — the only person who ever really understood me. I have never forgiven you for having her consigned to that — that nursing home."

"It was most necessary towards the end," rejoined his father. "I doubt whether, in her more lucid moments, she would like what you have become. You caused her worry enough — caused both of us great concern — while you were still quite a youngster. Now, release Judy from that bench you swine or I'll surely let you have both barrels of this shotgun, no matter what!"

"You wouldn't dare flout the law like that," scoffed his son. "You always have lived according to the book."

"Not any longer. I used this same shotgun on young Warren when I discovered that he had been responsible for Janet's death," the old man said levelly.

At this admission you could almost have cut the hush in that cellar with a knife.

"*You* — you killed Gary Warren?" said Tony Quinton incredulously.

"Oh, yes. I've long felt that in waiving the death penalty for murder we have been ill-advised. Warren killed my daughter so I killed Warren!"

Tony Quinton shook his head slowly in disbelief. "How did you discover that Gary killed Janet?"

"I made certain enquiries myself. I had my suspicions. When I faced him that evening with this gun he confessed quite freely."

"You can be tried for murder now."

"Perhaps, but as I've been told that I've only a short time to live, the thought doesn't worry me unduly."

His son smiled triumphantly. "So you're reaching the end of the road at last, and not before time. You had no compunction about putting me away for years because I had the audacity to break some of your stupid laws. What's helping you to a swift end, Father dear? Something painful like terminal cancer, I trust."

"No, you'll be disappointed to learn that it's only my heart. Disconcerting at times, but not excruciatingly painful, thanks to the tablets that Stephen keeps me supplied with. When he discovered that my pump was likely to cease functioning at any time, he told me that he could only help me borrow a few more months at the most."

"I'm afraid that dear little Stephen has used up all his own time. He ran into an unlucky bullet. This evening I was interrupted while making arrangements to have him buried in — er — non-consecrated ground."

"You've murdered Stephen?" The old man's face drained of colour.

"An unlucky occurrence, Father dear. Certainly nothing like so intentional as when I secretly fed some hallucinatory drugs to your dear second wife and then encouraged her to go riding."

"You did what?"

"Oh, it was something I had planned on and off for quite some time. I was already experimenting with various drugs. The combination I fed dear step-mother was most successful."

"How could you bring yourself to do such a monstrous thing, Tony?"

"Quite easily. You never really had

much time for my mother after the war. Oh, yes, I now know all about the Anglo-Burmese nurse you got with child during your latter-day spell with the 14th Army in Rangoon. You couldn't marry her because you had already contracted one of those hasty war-time marriages back home here in England. But when Nursie died after the birth of your child you quietly arranged for the boy to be brought back here and adopted by a local couple. That's the real reason why Stephen Grant was always your favourite. And the reason why I'm so glad that he's dead now."

"You've killed every one I've ever truly loved, except Judy," said the old Judge, heavily.

I braced myself as I saw the knuckle of his trigger-finger whiten.

18

"DON'T do anything hasty, Father dear," said Tony Quinton, shifting the aim of the automatic he held so that it covered Judy. "My reflexes are a mite quicker than yours. You pull that trigger and I'll send this dear step-sister to keep company with the rest of her family."

All eyes were on the old man, face drained of colour, lower lip trembling, but that shotgun still aimed steadily at his son. For the moment Andy and I were forgotten.

"There's a knife on that shelf beside you," I whispered to the youngster, who had recovered sufficiently to pull himself to his feet and was all but leaning against me. "Move slowly. See if you can cut this rope at my wrists."

Seconds later, while father and son still glared at each other, I felt the knife begin to saw at my bonds — slipping once or twice to gnaw at my flesh instead.

"Let me take over the shotgun," I said to the Judge, as soon as my hands were free.

I could sense his relief as he carefully relinquished hold of the weapon. By now his face had the pallor of anaemic parchment, and no sooner had he passed the shotgun over than his first act was to transfer a couple of tablets from the pocket of the fawn car-coat that hung slackly on his gaunt frame and transfer them to his mouth with trembling fingers.

"Andy, keep well out of the line of fire, old son, and cut Judy free. As for you lot," I said, addressing our former captors who had had the bad sense to group themselves nicely together. "If just one of you steps out of line or moves a hand I'll turn your faces into bloody pulp. And you've no idea what pleasure that would afford me."

"Surely you're a reasonable man,"

said Tony Quinton, almost affably. "I have the means to make everyone here, yourself included, rich beyond your wildest dreams."

"By peddling drugs?" I said, watching carefully while Andy finished cutting Judy free.

"Does the means matter?" he replied. "During my sojourn out East I discovered a fungi — worshipped by an aboriginal tribe as much for its phallic symbolism as for the hallucinatory effects it produces when eaten in even minute quantities. It took all my skill plus the help of a Belgian pharmacologist to obtain a soluble drug from the fungi that could be combined with heroin in such a way that it produced one of the most powerful and addictive drugs imaginable."

"Mega-H?" I said.

"I understand that's the street name by which it is called."

"And this cellar — this growing room — is to enable you to cultivate this tropical fungus right here?"

"You're most perceptive: that's exactly what we intend to do," he admitted. "Scarlet-cap fungus, as I have named it, had probably never been discovered by outsiders; it's certainly never been reported in the Western world. Unfortunately the natives were far from friendly. They were most uncooperative, in fact, when it came to harvesting a few of their precious fungi for our own purposes. But my Belgian colleague demonstrated how simple it was to grow Scarlet-cap, providing the conditions are right. Our early attempts were in Hong Kong, but a Chinese Triad took exception to our efforts to break into their market and simply put a torch to our place and burnt us out." His hand touched the paper-thin scar-tissue on his face, as he added, "Not all of us escaped scot-free from that blaze."

"The heat and humidity you've achieved down here are sufficient for the establishment of this fungus?" I said.

He nodded. "With a controlled growing set-up like this we have proved that Scarlet-cap can be nurtured from spore to mycelium and on to final ripening at an astonishing rate." He paused. "When I also tell you that through Laura Banks and certain other contacts we have completed the most gratifying connections with both Continental and American members of their respective Mafiosa you will readily understand what an unsurpassed distribution we will have for our product. I assure you, O'Hara, there is unlimited wealth just awaiting our full entry into world markets."

"You talk of wealth. How about those unfortunates who fall victim to this new drug you have produced?" put in Judy, bitterly, clutching the torn remnants of her blouse about her.

"I know all about the drug's side-effects," he shrugged. "Dear Janet already demonstrated its powerful addiction. It is that addiction that makes it such a money-spinner for us. In the end there was nothing that Janet wouldn't do to secure her next fix. She made such an admirable little guinea-pig for my experiments. We had her featuring in pornographic pictures — the lot!" He suddenly glared at Judy. "How I hated you two girls — just as I hated your mother. If you must know, you were to be my next guinea-pig, Judy dear. I had something really exciting in store for you — trying out a stronger compound to test its aphrodisiac powers to the full."

"How about the photographs that your friends tried to blackmail your father with?" I said.

"You mean the ones purporting to show Janet and Judy cavorting in a lesbian way together? They were fakes. A simple montage, taking advantage of Janet's likeness to her sister to use pictures of her twice in the same print. In a way it's a pity that Janet had to die so soon."

"But she had time to take her revenge, Tony," chimed in Laura

Banks, speaking up for the first time. "Even now we haven't been able to secure those Scarlet-cap spores that Louis d'Arville had flown across to us. She knew they were the last of the batch that you brought out of the jungle. I'm still not certain whether she stole them simply to spite you or to use as a bargaining power to ensure herself of a continuing supply of the drug."

Tony Quinton grimaced so that the scar-tissue on his face wrinkled alarmingly. "It was because she had a touch of conscience my dear Laura," he said. "She felt that she was doomed herself, no matter what. That's why she posted the package to dear Father's London address, with a note explaining the full significance of the spores. By the way, Father dear, has the package arrived at the house yet?"

"I'm saying nothing to you," snapped the old Judge, having recovered some of his vitality. "That young man there," he indicated Andy, 'phoned me when he saw what was happening. I've no doubt he then 'phoned the police."

"Hell, if that's true, we'd better clear out of here," put in Jimmy Luckin, in some alarm. "The three of us can easily slip back to the Continent. I always thought we had a much safer set-up there than here in this dead-and-alive hole. The plane's all fuelled up. Laura can pilot us just as well as that wop pilot you hired. In any case, he's in Gloucester now with the rest of the boys."

"Here, hold hard, sport," said Eddie Moxon, truculently. "If you three piss off just what's supposed to happen to Charlie, Marco, me, and the rest of the boys?"

"You can get word to the bunch in Gloucester, then nip down to London and so on to the coast," said Luckin, airily. "We'll meet up with you either in Brussels or at the Marseilles address."

"There's no need for anyone to panic," said Tony Quinton calmly. "If our dusky young friend had 'phoned the police, I'm sure we would have heard from them by now. Providing we can dispose of these people as speedily as possible, there'll be nothing for the police to prove even should they eventually turn up here. After all, there's no law in this country that forbids the growing of fungi. I defy anyone to discover how I succeeded in extracting the hallucinatory drug in such a way that it readily combines with heroin that can then be injected in soluble form. Our other concern is to rid ourselves of the contents of that trunk in the small lab and then make quite sure that every last grain of our heroin stock is well out of reach of the prying eyes of the law."

"And how do you propose to rid ourselves of this lot?" Luckin asked, waving a cigar in our direction.

"We'll take care of them," his companion said serenely.

"I can't bloody well see how, Boss," put in Moxon. "I for one don't wanta argue with that friggin' shotgun. No sir! No way!"

"That gun has only two barrels," said Tony Quinton quietly. "Although there are four of them that's the only weapon they've got. Now there are six of us and we each carry a gun. Even dear Laura is probably sporting that little pearl-handled shooter she's so fond of."

"If any of your chums so much as reach for their guns now, Quinton, I'll make sure that I present you — and you alone — with both barrels," I chimed in. "Lord knows you're no oil-painting at the moment, but a double dose of buckshot at this range will loosen your head from your body."

His thin lips crawled to a sneer. "I'm not at all sure that you will fire that gun," he said. "Take note that this automatic is still covering my dear step-sister. Blast me and the nervous reaction of my finger on this trigger will assuredly be enough to pump two or three bullets into her."

"Perhaps my reflexes will be much quicker than yours," I countered.

He grinned evilly. "Perhaps, dear boy. Feel like putting it to the test?"

It certainly appeared to be stalemate, I glanced quickly at my companions. Andy Richards, hands balled into fists, dusky jaw-line tense, stood glowering at the opposition; Judy, calmly erect, one hand closing the torn blouse across her breasts; and the Judge, face ashen again, hands thrust deep into the patch pockets of his car coat.

It was the old man who spoke, having first cleared his throat with a dry cough.

"Tony, were you exaggerating when you told us that you had been responsible for your step-mother's death?"

"Of course not, Father dear! Let me present the matter in detail. As a judge you will appreciate how easily I was able to get away with murder. First, you must know that there are certain hallucinogenic fungi that are native to this country. Some of us at University nicknamed them 'Happy Toadstools'. In the early days of religion here, I believe the druids knew the power of these things, and employed them to good effect. Well, at a time when you were attending a protracted case at the Old Bailey, and the two girls were at their respective seats of learning, I returned to the family bosom. In point of fact I had been sent down from University for a youthful peccadillo. Immediately, I had to submit to receiving one hell of a lecture from dear step-mother, about improving my behaviour for your sake, Father dear. A couple of days of this was enough for me, and when one morning she surprised me with a village girl in my bedroom, trying to encourage the wench to open her legs even wider, she blew her top. Breakfast that morning consisted of a grill with mushrooms. I saw to it that among her mushrooms were a fair quantity of Happy Toadstools, with a judicious sprinkling of lysergic acid as an added condiment, just to help things along. That morning I watched her gradually becoming higher and higher. By mid-morning when she was all set to take her usual morning canter she must have thought she could fly. Certainly by the time she was in the saddle she was as high as a kite ... Such a pity, Father dear, that she left her saddle so abruptly and stove her head in. Of course, with the cause of death so plain to see there wasn't much need for a detailed autopsy ... " he suddenly paused, and stared with disbelieving eyes at his father.

Like some gaunt, stooped magician, the old man had produced a heavy Service revolver from his car-coat pocket. Even as Tony Quinton automatically swung the muzzle of his own weapon to cover his father, the Service pistol barked once and as it struck home the force of that heavy bullet swung the younger man off balance so that the stream of bullets that immediately issued from his own automatic stitched a neat little line across some piled sacks of horticultural peat stacked to one side of the cellar.

Laura Banks dropped to her knees beside the fallen man. "My God, he's dead!" she wailed. "You old bastard, you've shot him through the heart — killed your own son!"

"It's a well-merited death," Judge Quinton said heavily, left-hand raised to massage the heart-region of his own body. "It's many years since I fired that revolver. I've always looked after it. In Burma it dealt out capital punishment more than once to certain Japanese gentlemen whom we had caught torturing some of our lads."

Unexpected though it had been, the shock of Tony's killing was just the break I needed. None of the opposition had taken the opportunity to draw their own weapons. Now they were menaced by the shotgun and the Service revolver.

"The first one who so much as twitches a muscle will get a barrel of this straight in the face," I panned the shotgun threateningly. "Andy, I think you had better take over the revolver from the Judge. Don't hesitate to use it." And as the youngster took possession of the Judge's weapon and trained it in a commendably workmanlike fashion at the remaining five villains, I said to them, "I think you must realise that the game's up. Let's have all your weapons dropped on the floor in front of you." As they grudgingly complied with this reasonable request, I further ordered that they kick the various guns across in our direction.

"Right, Judy, pick up any shooter you fancy. Not that little pearl-handled toy. It hasn't enough stopping power unless you're at very close range. Try that Walthers. Good, now nip over to that telephone there," I indicated a wall-mounted instrument in a far corner. "Get through to Inspector Marlow. You can still keep an eye on these birds in case one or the other tries to get saucy." I turned to the Judge, now slumped rather than seated on the edge of a work-bench, breathing in a distressingly shallow fashion. "Are you all right, sir?"

"I'll last long enough to see these scum taken into custody. It's a pity that I'll not be able to preside at their trial."

I glanced to where his son's body lay. "It must have cost you, but justice was done, tonight, you know."

The old man nodded. "Stephen Grant was always more of a son to me than that one lying there, although Stephen was the illegitimate boy."

I shot Andy Richards a quick glance. He noticed it and his teeth gleamed in his dark features. Maybe that chip on his shoulder wouldn't rest quite so heavily after tonight's work.

Judy succeeded in raising the fuzz and rejoined Andy and me. Although the minutes we had to wait for the arrival of the law seemed like so many hours, with three weapons menacing them none of the opposition showed signs of becoming heroic.

It was Inspector Marlow who led his merry men down the stone steps and into the cellar. "Hmph!" he said, with an eye to the prone body of Tony Quinton. "It looks as though we have a nice little bag here, O'Hara. As usual, you'll want us to tidy up all the loose ends in our own humble way." Then, glancing towards Judge Quinton who was by now in a state of near collapse, he added, "Sergeant, get on to the hospital. I want an ambulance out here straight away."

"I don't know how many men you brought with you, Inspector," I put in. "But another party of villains are expected back from Gloucester, presumably either tonight or tomorrow morning. I think a quietly placed reception committee would be in order."

Marlow's eyes definitely twinkled. "The more the merrier," he said. "Right, Sergeant, after you've 'phoned the hospital, get through to Baker, back at the Station. Tell him to round up every available man — uniformed and plain-clothed — and I want 'em here sooner than now!"

"Y'know, all this is quite unnecessary, Inspector," Jimmy Luckin chimed in, obviously hoping his luck hadn't deserted him. "My friends and I were discussing a business venture down here when this ruffian and his accomplices crashed in. As a direct result my partner was murdered in cold blood, and the rest of us were threatened unless we paid out a vast sum in ransom." And having delivered himself of this little fairy story, he calmly lit up another cigar.

"That's as may be," rejoined Marlow, acidly. "Meanwhile I must ask you and your — er — friends to accompany me to the Station."

"On what charge, Inspector?" demanded Luckin, insolently.

"Perhaps we'll think of something on the way," replied the Inspector. "So, if you don't mind, sir . . . " and he indicated the steps leading to the great wide world outside.

"Oh, if you insist," said Luckin, beginning to lead his companions from the cellar.

As he drew level with me, something about the smug look on his fleshy face, the sight of that expensive cigar being enjoyed with such ostentation, and memory of his obvious delight in burning Judy's breast, caused the O'Hara temper to slip its collar. Transferring the Smith & Wesson to my left hand, I took a full-blooded right-hand punch and had the pleasure of feeling my fist smash into his oily face, quite ruining his cigar and sending at least three front incisors to ricochet off his tonsils. He landed rather heavily on his backside, and I was about to coax him to his feet with a goal-scoring kick when I was halted by sight of Inspector Marlow's censorious look.

Spitting blood and invective, I thought our Jimmy was about to launch himself at me when he finally prised his arse off the cellar floor — but no such luck.

"You saw what that — bastard — just did to me, Inspector," he mouthed.

"A most unfortunate accident, sir," said Marlow smoothly. "This cellar floor is quite slippery in places. Mister O'Hara must have lost his footing for a moment — just as you did. Now sir, will you lead the way? You'll find a large dark blue van waiting to receive you in the drive outside."

19

WHAT little remained of that night, Judy and I spent together. It was not the time for the more passionate moments of love, just her need to have someone hold her close. When she finally fell asleep in my arms, it was like holding a disturbed child, the strain of past events visible in the pale set of features that should have been serene in slumber. But by the next morning she was her own composed self again, greeting me with a warm embrace.

Breakfast was late. Immediately afterwards I put a call through to Inspector Marlow, who must have spent a busy night, but whose voice was as cool and crisp as though he'd had his regulation eight-hours sleep. He assured me that my presence wasn't needed again at the Station, for that day at least. My next call was to the Gnome, who appeared strangely excited and expressed a desire, couched in rather Anglo-Saxon terms, to see me just as soon as I could get my posterior moving in his direction.

First, however, Judy and I called in at the hospital to see how her step-father was faring. After a massive heart attack he was in an intensive care unit, with stubborn tenacity still refusing to release hold of the last frail thread of life. Should he recover, I wondered how he would face up to the resultant publicity of the nightmare events in Jimmy Luckin's farmhouse cellar. The early national newspapers had either not yet received the story — or it had come through so late that they'd had insufficient time to stop the presses. But when the story finally broke I could visualise the banner headlines: JUDGE SHOOTS OWN SON . . . COTSWOLD DRUG RING BROKEN . . . BRUTAL MURDERS EXPLAINED, and so on.

"Do you mind if I stay on here for a while?" said Judy, looking down at her step-father. Sister says that he may rally. Should he regain consciousness I'd like to be here with him. He was always extremely good to me. No matter that he took the law into his own hands, I wouldn't want him to think that I've deserted him now."

"Of course. I'll pop round to see what's biting the Gnome, but I'll keep my visit as short as possible. Stay on here at the hospital until I return."

Fifteen minutes later, Sir Norman Norrick greeted me in his own inimitable fashion when I hove to on his horizon — or rather walked into that splendid book-lined study of his.

"You took your time getting here, O'Hara."

"One or two things to sort out. You'll have heard about last night's affair."

"I have, but it wouldn't have come amiss to have received the bloody news from you rather than Marlow. Christ, you *are* supposed to be our man in the field."

"Didn't think you'd thank me for waking you at that time of night."

"I can't say that sod, Marlow, had such qualms. However, from what he tells me you appear to have acquitted yourself reasonably well over this little Cotswold episode. That's one reason why I've sent for you this morning. Something really big has just cropped up. It means slipping over to Pakistan or, maybe, Kashmir for a time, but I know just how keen you'll be to get started when I tell you what's entailed."

"You can stop right there!" I snarled. "What's the matter with that index-file you call a memory? I promised to see this last job through but after that, as I told you, I'm finished with INIT. Dammit, you know I've made other plans!"

"Quite so, quite so! I remember all that, m'boy," the Gnome said placidly. "You wish to marry Miss Quinton.

Now this little job that's just come up will make it so much easier for you and your intended. I'm only offering you this chance because I have so much faith in your ability — and the bonus would make such a fine wedding present."

"Bonus?" It was news to me that any members of the INIT team were ever in line for a bonus.

"Exactly, m'boy. I knew you'd be interested. We pay our operatives reasonably, but any young fellow-me-lad who's thinking of getting spliced needs a little boost in the bank to help cover — ah — initial expenses of honeymoon and household. Eh?"

"All right, tell me all about it," I said resignedly. "But the answer will be 'No' in the end, I assure you."

"Oh, quite! I'll understand, m'boy. But just listen to this: a new opium-boss has reared his bloody ugly head, this time in Pakistan. He has hit upon the idea of cutting out middleman profits by selling direct to the governments of the Western world. He reckons on having up to one half of the world's supply of opium ready either for destruction or pushing out to his normal contacts, depending on how his offer is received. He maintains that by good husbandry he is able to harvest some 300 tons of opium a year. Now that amount of opium can be turned into 30 tons of heroin. At street prices currently prevailing this could net something like 150,000 million pounds sterling."

"He's following in the footsteps of those two wily birds, Lo Sing Han and his rival, Kun Sar. They both tried to make deals with the U.S. Government," I said. "As I remember it, Lo Sing Han was prepared to sell about one-third of the world's illegal supply of opium for a mere 12 million dollars American, but through a certain amount of skulduggery, this self-styled 'King of Opium' was arrested, extradited to Burma and sentenced to death for treason. Kun Sar, commander of the

Shan Army of irregulars also tried for secret negotiations with the U.S. Government. The final instalment of that little deal, as I recall it, was the Thais giving him the ultimatum of either moving his army out of Thailand and leaving his productive fields or they would blast him and his convoys to Kingdom Come with bombing attacks."

"Your memory serves you well, m'boy," the Gnome said. "But this new opium warlord seems determined to chance his arm at the same game. He has offered to allow an international team, including members of INIT to supervise the destruction of this year's crop — providing we pay for it."

"How much? Half the contents of Fort Knox?" I scoffed.

"Not quite, m'boy, just a specified amount in industrial diamonds — at a gross value of 20 million dollars. I expect they'll be flogged to the Chinese government for at least three times their normal value. We've had it on the grapevine that industrial diamonds are the 'in' thing at the moment."

"That amount in gold would be too bulky and heavy for easy transport," I said. "These days it would appear to be over-rated as a currency for shady deals."

"True enough," agreed the Gnome. "The latest figures I've had from States' side show that cocaine is now fetching three times its own weight in gold. This, of course is where the Triads have been unable to compete for that opium harvest. They can offer gold or any currency that one might care to name, but industrial diamonds to that tune would take them too bloody long to garner together — and our Opium Princeling is clamouring for speedy action. It's harvest-time in them thar hills."

"So the Triads are trying to muscle in on these deal?" I said.

"Oh, no, m'boy. Those little Oriental buggers are well out of the running, as I've explained."

"What I know of them, they're never to be counted out of the running so far as any drug deals are concerned."

"Not this time, O'Hara. They simply can't come up with the gelt in time."

"And where d'you figure on fitting me into all this?" I asked.

"Ah, yes! Well, the fact of the matter is that some careless bloody clot has lost us the industrial diamonds, y'see."

"No, I don't see. So far I thought the dialogue had all been in the future tense. Do you mean to say that the deal is already under way?"

The Gnome sighed. "We wish it was, m'boy. We really do. The diamonds are due to be handed over in a week's time. No diamonds — no deal! Then, I've no doubt some other unscrupulous bastards will step in. Other big boys of the drug caper must have got wind of the deal by now. If it goes through their own trade will be severely bloody hamstrung."

"Christ, man you'll have all the eastern thugs, plus the Triads, breathing down the neck of anyone who's stupid enough to try to rescue this mission."

"Oh, come now, surely you're over-dramatizing the situation?" my diminutive boss suggested, delicately fingering the lobe of one of his little shell-likes. "And then, there's the incentive of that bonus I mentioned."

"About the bonus, just where does that figure in the nature of things?" I said.

"It's a specified sum of money that the Western governments have agreed to pay to those who recover the diamonds and then see the whole deal go through as planned," the Gnome smiled happily. "That was why I immediately thought of you, m'boy, and your probable need for a little more cash in the jolly old coffers."

"Anyone who comes up against members of the Triads or some of the other rival drug gangs are likely to get the chopper in the same spot that the chicken got it — never mind about cash in the coffers," I replied sourly.

"But it's such a large bonus," protested the gnome. "Surely some small risk is worth that?"

"How much, exactly — not the risk, but the bonus?"

"One percent of the gross total of those diamonds."

"Doesn't sound all that much to me," I answered, glossing over the simple maths involved.

"I think it's remarkably good reward for what may well be a pleasant trip out East," said the Gnome firmly. "Just remove the last two noughts from the original twenty million dollars and you are left with . . . "

"Jesus, two hundred thousand dollars!"

The Gnome eyed me speculatively, aware that cupidity was beginning to take over. "How would you like to mention this small matter to Miss Quinton some time today? 'Phone me with your affirmative answer, this evening, m'boy."

"How do you know I will agree to go?"

"Because both Judy Quinton and yourself are eminently practical people," said the Gnome suavely. "I know they say that money doesn't buy happiness, but take it from me, m'boy, it helps to smooth out most of the furrows of life."

"Always supposing I've any life left after this trip."

"'Phone me this evening," was the little cherub's smiling reply.

★ ★ ★

"Does that burn still hurt?" I asked Judy, when I saw her later that day.

"It's not too painful now. Sister at the hospital applied some soothing salve that has taken my mind off it, as you might say," she smiled.

"How's the old Judge?" I asked.

"He rallied for a while. Saw me and recognised me, then lapsed into unconsciousness again. I'll let you take me to lunch now."

"Will that burn leave a scar?" I asked later, having seen off a very appetizing veal escalõp at a local hostelry.

Judy gave me a quizzical look. "The state of my breast seems to worry you, Michael."

Under the table my hands balled into fists. "I can still see that — that swine — burning you," I said.

One of her hands reached across to touch mine. "It's done with now, Michael. If it does scar, and you find it too off-putting I'll have to consider plastic surgery, I suppose," she smiled.

"Oh, I'm certain our progeny won't find it off-putting. They'll be too concerned with their nourishment."

She laughed. "How do you know I believe in breast-feeding?"

"It would be such a waste of superb equipment if you didn't. By the way, have I ever mentioned the frequent incident of twins in the O'Hara clan?"

She looked at me fondly. "I could

put up with that, if you could — just so long as careless gentlemen don't keep using me for an ash-tray. And speaking of carelessness, did you have to be quite so severe in dealing with Mr. Luckin? You spoilt his cigar."

"Given the chance I'll ruin more than that for him," I said, savagely.

"Well, never mind all that now," Judy said. "You still haven't told me what Sir Norman wanted to see you about."

I drained my glass of wine, best house white, took a deep breath and told her all. At the end she was silent for several minutes, then:

"I've heard that Kashmir is a wonderful place — ideal for a honeymoon," she said. "I can always take some artists' materials along so that I can busy myself while you are attending to INIT's work."

"If I take this job on, you won't be accompanying me."

There and then, in front of several surprised onlookers, she demonstrated her appetite by throwing an arm about my neck, pulling me close and nibbling at my ear.

"I know you really want to go on this one, Michael. 'Phone Sir Norman now and tell him you'll take it on. Don't wait for this evening. I've other plans for you then. All this talk of babies has made me quite broody."

THE END

Other titles in the
Linford Mystery Library:

A GENTEEL LITTLE MURDER
Philip Daniels

Gilbert had a long-cherished plan to murder his wife. When the polished Edward entered the scene Gilbert's attitude was suddenly changed.

DEATH AT THE WEDDING
Madelaine Duke

Dr. Norah North's search for a killer takes her from a wedding to a private hospital.

MURDER FIRST CLASS
Ron Ellis

Will Detective Chief Inspector Glass find the Post Office robbers before the Executioner gets to them?

A FOOT IN THE GRAVE
Bruce Marshall

About to be imprisoned and tortured in Buenos Aires, John Smith escapes, only to become involved in an aeroplane hijacking.

DEAD TROUBLE
Martin Carroll

Trespassing brought Jennifer Denning more than she bargained for. She was totally unprepared for the violence which was to lie in her path.

HOURS TO KILL
Ursula Curtiss

Margaret went to New Mexico to look after her sick sister's rented house and felt a sharp edge of fear when the absent landlady arrived.

THE DEATH OF ABBE DIDIER
Richard Grayson

Inspector Gautier of the Sûreté investigates three crimes which are strangely connected.

NIGHTMARE TIME
Hugh Pentecost

Have the missing major and his wife met with foul play somewhere in the Beaumont Hotel, or is their disappearance a carefully planned step in an act of treason?

BLOOD WILL OUT
Margaret Carr

Why was the manor house so oddly familiar to Elinor Howard? Who would have guessed that a Sunday School outing could lead to murder?

THE DRACULA MURDERS
Philip Daniels

The Horror Ball was interrupted by a spectral figure who warned the merrymakers they were tampering with the unknown.

THE LADIES
OF LAMBTON GREEN
Liza Shepherd

Why did murdered Robin Colquhoun's picture pose such a threat to the ladies of Lambton Green?

CARNABY
AND THE GAOLBREAKERS
Peter N. Walker

Detective Sergeant James Aloysius Carnaby-King is sent to prison as bait. When he joins in an escape he is thrown headfirst into a vicious murder hunt.

MUD IN HIS EYE
Gerald Hammond

The harbourmaster's body is found mangled beneath Major Smyle's yacht. What is the sinister significance of the illicit oysters?

THE SCAVENGERS
Bill Knox

Among the masses of struggling fish in the *Tecta*'s nets was a larger, darker, ominously motionless form . . . the body of a skin diver.

DEATH IN ARCADY
Stella Phillips

Detective Inspector Matthew Furnival works unofficially with the local police when a brutal murder takes place in a caravan camp.

STORM CENTRE
Douglas Clark

Detective Chief Superintendent Masters, temporarily lecturing in a police staff college, finds there's more to the job than a few weeks relaxation in a rural setting.

THE MANUSCRIPT MURDERS
Roy Harley Lewis

Antiquarian bookseller Matthew Coll, acquires a rare 16th century manuscript. But when the Dutch professor who had discovered the journal is murdered, Coll begins to doubt its authenticity.

SHARENDEL
Margaret Carr

Ruth didn't want all that money. And she didn't want Aunt Cass to die. But at Sharendel things looked different. She began to wonder if she had a split personality.

MURDER TO BURN
Laurie Mantell

Sergeants Steven Arrow and Lance Brendon, of the New Zealand police force, come upon a woman's body in the water. When the dead woman is identified they begin to realise that they are investigating a complex fraud.

YOU CAN HELP ME
Maisie Birmingham

Whilst running the Citizens' Advice Bureau, Kate Weatherley is attacked with no apparent motive. Then the body of one of her clients is found in her room.

DAGGERS DRAWN
Margaret Carr

Stacey Manston was the kind of girl who could take most things in her stride, but three murders were something different . . .

THE MONTMARTRE MURDERS
Richard Grayson

Inspector Gautier of Sûreté investigates the disappearance of artist Théo, the heir to a fortune.

GRIZZLY TRAIL
Gwen Moffat

Miss Pink, alone in the Rockies, helps in a search for missing hikers, solves two cruel murders and has the most terrifying experience of her life when she meets a grizzly bear!

BLINDMAN'S BLUFF
Margaret Carr

Kate Deverill had considered suicide. It was one way out — and preferable to being murdered.

BEGOTTEN MURDER
Martin Carroll

When Susan Phillips joined her aunt on a voyage of 12,000 miles from her home in Melbourne, she little knew their arrival would germinate the seeds of murder planted long ago.

WHO'S THE TARGET?
Margaret Carr

Three people whom Abby could identify as her parents' murderers wanted her dead, but she decided that maybe Jason could have been the target.

THE LOOSE SCREW
Gerald Hammond

After a motor smash, Beau Pepys and his cousin Jacqueline, her fiancé and dotty mother, suspect that someone had prearranged the death of their friend. But who, and why?

SPECIAL MESSAGE TO READERS

This book is published under the auspices of
THE ULVERSCROFT FOUNDATION
(registered charity No. 264873 UK)

Established in 1972 to provide funds for research, diagnosis and treatment of eye diseases. Examples of contributions made are: —

A new Children's Assessment Unit at Moorfield's Hospital, London.

Twin operating theatres at the Western Ophthalmic Hospital, London.

A Chair of Ophthalmology at the University of Leicester.

The establishment of a Royal Australian College of Ophthalmologists "Fellowship".

You can help further the work of the Foundation by making a donation or leaving a legacy. Every contribution, no matter how small, is received with gratitude. Please write for details to:

**THE ULVERSCROFT FOUNDATION,
The Green, Bradgate Road, Anstey,
Leicester LE7 7FU, England.
Telephone: (0116) 236 4325**

**In Australia write to:
THE ULVERSCROFT FOUNDATION,
c/o The Royal Australian College of
Ophthalmologists,
27, Commonwealth Street, Sydney,
N.S.W. 2010.**

LP   Jackson, Charles.
F
JACKSON The Cotswold connection

PROPERTY OF
Navajo County Library D
100 E. Carter Dr., PO Box
Holbrook, AZ 86025

DEMCO 38-296